GLYNETTE'S CORPORAL

GLYNETTE'S CORPORAL

•

Gena Cline

AVALON BOOKS
NEW YORK

© Copyright 2005 by Gena Brandvold
Library of Congress Catalog Card Number: 2004099740
ISBN 0-8034-9727-X
All rights reserved.
All the characters in this book are fictitious,
and any resemblance to actual persons,
living or dead, is purely coincidental.
Published by Thomas Bouregy & Co., Inc.
160 Madison Avenue, New York, NY 10016

PRINTED IN THE UNITED STATES OF AMERICA
ON ACID-FREE PAPER
BY HADDON CRAFTSMEN, BLOOMSBURG, PENNSYLVANIA

For Pete, of course.

Chapter One

As the train eased into the Harding depot, Glynette McCrae scraped her gloved fingernails over the icy window until a small, clear spot formed. As she peered through it, her heart sank.

"It's dreadful," she murmured, "even worse than Anniston described."

"You got that right, sister."

Startled, she jumped and turned her gaze toward the shriveled, white-haired man sitting across from her. He had been staring at her silently for the past four hours.

"Good heavens," she exclaimed, her nerves raw. "I had assumed you were deaf."

Blinking his rheumy blue eyes, the old man added, "Harding makes Gomorrah look like a bastion of God-fearing, wholesome living."

Glynette pulled her wide-eyed gaze from the peculiar man back to the ramshackle array of crude huts outside the train window. She suspected the man was right. According to her husband, Harding existed only to provide cowboys, soldiers, and railroad laborers with booze and pleasure girls. Worse, it was the only town within a hundred miles of Fort Reynolds, her new home.

Pressing her cheek to the window, she stared with dread at the trackless land beyond the depot.

The end of the line.

Nothing but wolves, Indians, and outlaws beyond this point. And, of course, Fort Reynolds.

The train blew its mournful whistle. Brakes groaning, it gave a final lurch forward and stopped. On the platform, a burly, bearded man, who managed to look unkempt even in uniform, lumbered back and forth alongside the train, craning his neck to see the passengers inside. He reached Glynette's car just as she stepped into the doorway.

"Mrs. McCrae, thank God!" Grasping her waist, the big man swung her easily to the platform.

"Gregor!" Glynette shouted above the wind. She threw her arms around the thick, bristly neck of her old friend. "How strange to see you in this strange place!" She leaned her head back and gazed at him through tears, choking on the lump in her throat. "But I am so glad to see you."

"Likewise, Mrs. McCrae."

Blinking back the tears, Glynette laughed. Though he'd been a family friend since she was in pigtails, Gregor Britzman insisted on calling her Mrs. McCrae. She was, after all, his captain's wife. He could never hide the fond twinkle in his eye, however, because to him she would always be that impish ten-year-old who loved to braid his horse's mane with ribbons.

Staggered by a blast of wind, Glynette caught her hat with one hand and held on to Gregor with the other. She glanced around the platform. "Where's Anniston?"

"Captain McCrae couldn't leave the fort!" Gregor shouted. "This storm's wreaked havoc." He pulled her arm through his. "Let's get you to someplace warm!"

Glynette's Corporal 3

She resisted his tug. "I want to go to Fort Reynolds straight away."

"In this weather?" Gregor shouted. "I think not! We'll get you to a hotel."

Jerking her arm loose, Glynette narrowed her blue eyes at him. "Don't argue with a tired, frozen woman, Gregor. I didn't spend six days crossing the country and twenty-four hours stalled on a cold train in a blizzard to spend the night in a hotel less than ten miles from the fort."

She was homesick and lonely, exhausted and shivering. She felt an almost panicked need to see her husband, to have him hold her and whisper tender, reassuring words in her ear. She had to know if anything remained of her marriage.

Gregor nodded solemnly. "I'm glad to see you're stubborn as ever, Glynette. That's a trait that will bode well for you in this harsh country."

While Gregor tucked Glynette into a sleigh piled with buffalo robes, two soldiers—one tall, broad-shouldered, and clean shaven, the other shorter with a long, shaggy mustache—held their mounts steady a few feet away. The mustached one touched his cap and gazed at Glynette with open admiration.

Glynette smiled and turned away.

Gregor laughed. "I think Scully is already smitten with you, Mrs. McCrae. You'd best get used to having a whole garrison of admirers."

Gregor shook his head and whistled under his breath. Yes, indeed. Glynette McCrae was a beauty who turned heads even in Washington, a city chockful of beauties. Most of these country lads had never seen such a woman. If a man wasn't beguiled by her soft curves and full bosom, he'd be in love when his eyes reached her angelic face. Atop a pale, slender neck, the finely chiseled features of her face were framed by a rich crown of braided black hair. Dark, union-blue eyes lifted in a sweep of heavy lashes above full lips that curved readily into a smile.

As he climbed into the sleigh, Gregor stole a sidelong glance at her. Fortunately for Fort Reynolds, the captain's wife was straight and true. Some women liked to drive men crazy just for sport. But Mrs. McCrae, absorbed by the bustle on the loading ramp, was not interested in tormenting the soldiers at all. In fact, she seemed oblivious to her effect.

"Let's get you home," Gregor said as he took up the reins. To the tall soldier, he said, "We're set, Tom."

Before Gregor could rein the mules away, the clatter of a wagon sounded from up the street. Looking behind her, Glynette saw a buckboard round a corner and head toward them. The driver was a big, grinning man with a brushy mustache and red cheeks. The box was crammed full of men. From illustrations she'd seen in magazines, Glynette knew they were cowboys. Dressed in mackinaws and scarves wrapped over their hats and tied beneath their chins, they were whooping and yelling and screaming epithets at ladies passing on the boardwalk. One of the men tipped back a bottle.

Drunk, Glynette thought. But the thought had no sooner crossed her mind than the wheel of the buckboard full of cowboys clipped the wheel of another wagon parked in front of the loading ramp. The wagon with the cowboys lurched sideways and continued down the street while the other wagon plunged onto its back left axle. Its wheel lay in the street.

Someone screamed.

Gregor yelled, "Hey!" But the wagonload of cowboys didn't slow down.

The two soldiers dismounted their horses and ran to the

wagon with the clipped wheel. "Here," Gregor said, handing her the reins. Then he was on the ground, too, running to the wagon.

Frowning, holding the reins tight in her gloved hand, Glynette peered into the gathering crowd. Then she saw what the commotion was about. A man was pinned beneath the wagon!

The soldiers scrambled around the wagon. The trapped man was reaching out with his arms and screaming. Glynette muffled a cry when she glimpsed the face of the man being crushed to death beneath his wagon. A contorted mask of human agony. Her muscles weakened, loosening her hold on the reins. The mules, feeling the slack, edged away from the commotion, and the sleigh slid forward.

Grasping the reins desperately, she avoided looking at the trapped man. She kept her eyes on Gregor and the two other men as they struggled to lift the wagon from the man's chest.

"She won't go!" Gregor yelled, winded. "We'll have to get the rest of those crates out of the bed."

"There's no time," Tom said. "He'll be dead by then." He turned toward the other man. "Nate! You come down here. Give me your spot."

They switched places, Tom moving to the wagon's exposed axle, Gregor and Nate to his left. Tom turned his back to the wagon, ripped off his coat, tossed it to the ground, and got a grip on the underside of the box.

"Heave!" he bellowed.

All three men heaved. Tom, facing Glynette, stretched his lips away from his teeth in a snarl. His eyes, squinted in pain and concentration, were glued to hers, unseeing. Glynette looked deep into the green eyes, tensing her body, lifting with him, willing her own strength into him. His face turned bright red. He gave a loud, animal growl as the wagon axle slowly lifted off the ground.

"Okay," he gasped, "Drag him out!"

"What? Tom, you can't—"

"Moooooove!"

The two men looked at each other, then scurried around Tom, bent down, and reached under the wagon. Each grabbed an arm of the man trapped beneath, then pulled. When the man was out, Gregor yelled, "Okay, let her go!"

Tom let the wagon fall, then reached up with his two long, broad arms to keep a crate from toppling from the box.

"Someone get the doc!" Gregor yelled.

"I'm here," said a man carrying a black bag, pushing his way impatiently through the crowd.

As Gregor and the other two soldiers stepped back, Glynette dropped her gaze to the man who had been trapped beneath the wagon. She saw that he was Chinese. He moaned and mumbled in his native tongue, jerking his head around in obvious pain, but there didn't appear to be any blood.

The doctor examined the man while Gregor and the two soldiers stood over them, watching, breath puffing in the chill air. "Okay, let's get him into my office—gently," the doctor said. "His sternum is crushed, and he has more than a few broken ribs."

The three men eased the groaning man onto a stretcher, lifted him, and moved slowly down the boardwalk. Glynette clutched the reins and stared after them.

"Welcome to Montana, Mrs. McCrae," she muttered with a shiver, and huddled deeper into the buffalo skins.

Five minutes later, Gregor and the other two soldiers returned. As the enlisted men mounted their horses, Gregor stepped into the sleigh, took the reins from her, and released the brake. To her unspoken question, he said, "A few broken ribs. He'll be all right." He shook the reins, and the mules plunged forward.

"Those men should be punished."

Gregor squinted his eyes against the blowing snow. "It's rough country, Mrs. McCrae."

The enlisted men fell in beside them, and Glynette looked up at the soldier who had saved the Chinaman's life. Exhausted and unnerved, she found his silhouette in the fading light reassuring. His bearing suggested safety, order, and civilization. He rode a coal-black, blazed-face stallion with white stockings, a more beautiful horse than enlisted men usually own. Sitting his mount easily, he moved in perfect unison with the graceful beast, his back straight, his strong shoulders held back.

He was handsome in a rugged way, she noticed, with a wide, full mouth and square, smooth-shaven jaw. Reaching down, he ran a gloved hand through the silky black mane and said some reassuring words to the horse that Glynette couldn't hear. *He represents all that is best in a cavalry soldier,* she thought, feeling an unexpected pride for the Frontier Army of which she was now a part.

The soldier turned to her, as if he knew she had been admiring him, and after a moment his lips parted in a good-natured grin, his green eyes crinkling at the corners. Turning away, she felt a blush burn through cheeks already reddened by the stinging cold. Her heart thumped heavily, and her head went light.

She must be delirious with cold and exhaustion, she thought. She hoped the soldier had not misunderstood her look. She did not think he had. There had been something unexpected in his eyes, a look of sorrow that belied his cool confidence. The look made her own loneliness and unhappiness momentarily seem less.

Still, one never knew what ideas a soldier might get

about a woman, so she kept her eyes trained forward until the soldier had pulled ahead to show the way.

As the last of Harding's scattered shacks disappeared behind them, Glynette wondered how they would find Fort Reynolds in the wilderness of white that surrounded them. Then she realized they were following the faint outlines of telegraph poles, one by one, like a single row of dead, limbless trees.

As her eyes swept the unbroken slate of white around her, she steeled her heart against despair. A few days ago, safe in her mother's Washington home, inspired by the romance of April breezes and cherry blossoms, she had been impatient to join her husband. Now, in the stark, wintry reality of Montana, she felt bewildered and alone.

Would Anniston be glad to see her? Could they still forge a happy marriage together? She prayed that they might, though their first two years together had shown little promise. Had it only been two years?

They had met at an Army gala. Anniston, struck by Glynette's beauty, pursued her boldly. To everyone around them, they seemed a perfect match. She was a striking beauty with a prestigious family name. He was a wealthy and ambitious West Point graduate.

Glynette did not object to Anniston's visits, as they seemed to please her father, himself an old Army hero, but she did not pretend to be interested in Anniston's courtship. She had no interest in marriage. Caring for her aging parents and single-handedly maintaining the beautiful, labyrinthine garden of her family's crumbling estate kept her busy and contented. Moreover, she had learned years ago that the philosophers and poets dwelling in her father's library were more stimulating company than foolish men enthralled by her beauty.

Perpetually absorbed by her studies in the garden or in

front of the fire, she showed little sympathy for the parade of suitors who attempted to court her. Her indifference to suitors became increasingly distressing to her father, as his health was failing, and his fortune had dwindled to nothing. He desperately wanted to see his only daughter in a secure marriage before his death, and when Anniston proposed, he had pleaded with her to accept.

To fulfill her dying father's wish, Glynette had ignored the steady drum of doubt in her heart and accepted Anniston's proposal. Though she did not love Anniston, she respected him and had appreciated his strength and guidance during her father's illness. She hoped that love would come later.

They had married quickly for her father's sake, foregoing a proper engagement. Shortly after the wedding, Glynette realized the gravity of her mistake. Anniston's self-assurance, she quickly found, leaned dangerously toward arrogance. His gentle guidance became more and more like domination. Increasingly, he told her how to dress, who to see, and how to spend her time.

As the wife of an ambitious officer, she found she was required to keep a full social calendar of appointments with influential people and play hostess to a continual parade of officers, politicians, and ladies. She had to be seen in the latest fashions, be invited to the best houses, and conduct herself with impeccable manners. Her old friends, mostly a scruffy lot of poets, artists, and "strong-minded" women, didn't fit into Anniston's picture. One by one they began to drift away.

Anniston, for his part, became increasingly frustrated with Glynette, who seemed incapable of rising to the social heights required of the wife of a man of his ambition. Her striking beauty alone wasn't enough. She must have the grand manner of a great man's wife. Unfortunately, he found Glynette to be perversely bookish and introverted, preferring quiet afternoons of gardening and painting to political galas and afternoon tea with high-ranking officers' wives. He became disgruntled and openly expressed his dissatisfaction with her. Soon he quit showing her any affection at all.

Though she had tried to please him, Anniston's demands had worn on Glynette. She had been relieved when he accepted a post in Montana Territory. She hoped that by escaping Washington—a town preoccupied with dinner parties, gossip, ambition, and scandal—she and Anniston might make a fresh start. Perhaps out West, away from the bustle and cutthroat politics, they would find some common ground for love.

She closed her eyes against the stark landscape, the burning cold. At least out here, she reflected, she no longer had to worry about putting on a good face for her mother. Glynette had let her mother believe in her daughter's happiness. It had been difficult to hold her tongue while her mother marveled at the stylish, elegant lady Anniston McCrae had made out of her strong-willed daughter. But since her father's death, her mother had grown frail and pitiful. Glynette knew it would break her mother's heart, perhaps even kill her, to know the truth.

As Glynette said good-bye on the station platform, she had hidden her tears, though she knew it would likely be the last time she would see her mother. She had consoled herself with the thought that her mother would die believing her only daughter was happy.

Glynette choked back a sob. *What's happened to me?* she wondered, as the swooshing of the sled runners kept rhythm with her thoughts. At one time she had been fiercely independent and individualistic. At college she had taken courses in mathematics, philosophy, and other subjects considered unfit for women. She had insisted she would never marry. She planned to spend her life in her childhood home, tending the roses in her mother's garden and discussing books with her father.

Now she was married, her father was gone, and she was in a strange, frightening place called Montana. But self-pity would do her no good. She must somehow find a way to make her marriage work, to find a way to be as happy as her mother had hoped she would be.

As she tried to bolster and cheer herself with such thoughts, her face and feet grew increasingly numb. The bitter wind stung tears into her eyes and a rasping cough into her lungs. When the sun, pale and weak behind a lingering blanket of clouds, dropped beyond the horizon, she wondered if they would reach the fort by nightfall. She feared they would never find their way in the vast, starless night. Not wanting to betray her fears, she said nothing to Gregor. He appeared strained and worried himself, peering ahead in concentrated silence, his whiskers and eyelashes frozen white.

She drew strength from the shadowy form of the tall, broad-shouldered soldier who rode ahead of them, showing the way. She was on the frontier now, she reflected, and must learn courage. She was an Army wife. Nevertheless, she could not suppress a small moan of relief when at last they saw dim lights shining from the windows of Fort Reynolds.

The sentry waved them into the compound—a large, loosely formed rectangle of white clapboard houses and low-slung buildings. Their escorts turned their mounts and waited as the sleigh crossed the broad parade and halted at the end of a row of two-story houses fronted with narrow porches. A scruffy shepherd dog emerged from the gloam, ran up to the big soldier and sat down obediently as though he'd been instructed many times to do so, but he squirmed with excitement at seeing the man who was obviously his master.

"Stay, Dan," the man said quietly, and the dog calmed himself.

"These are the officers' quarters, Mrs. McCrae," Gregor informed her as he reined up. "You and Captain McCrae occupy the end quarters here, in the duplex with me and Lucy."

Gregor's wife was not a favorite of Glynette's, so this news didn't cheer her any. She felt a brief twinge of annoyance at Anniston for never having mentioned it in his letters. Before she could reply with the expected nicety, the door to the house opened, and Anniston McCrae stepped out.

"Glynette! My lovely pet! You're frozen to the bone!"

She forced her frozen cheeks into a smile. "Oh, no, this is nothing," she joked with as much enthusiasm as she could muster, "I'm an Army wife, after all."

"Good girl," he said, pushing away the buffalo robes and holding out his hand for her. Only an inch taller than she, with a slight build and delicate features, he was, nevertheless, handsome and bore himself with supreme confidence. Everyone said he and Glynette, with their dramatic contrasts, made a striking couple—his hair as fair as hers was dark; his eyes a clear, almost colorless blue, hers so deep in hue they sometimes appeared black.

With exaggerated care, he clutched her and guided her mincingly toward the door, instructing her at every step: "No, dear, step here. Careful, careful, my dear. Step here. Watch the ice there."

She could have made her way better without the fuss, but it was Anniston's habit to make a show of being a doting husband whenever they were in public. The pretense seemed particularly silly in this case, as his only audience was Gregor and the two mounted soldiers. Though they kept straight faces, Glynette sensed that the soldiers were amused by Anniston's display. She could feel Tom's eyes on her.

"Anniston, really, I can walk," she said, trying to keep the humor in her voice. "Let me go now."

As though he hadn't heard, her husband tightened his grip until her toes barely touched the ground. "Watch the steps, dear. The wind polishes them into sheets of ice."

Trying to ignore the soldiers, Glynette allowed Anniston to guide her into the house. She breathed a sigh of relief as she heard the door slam behind her. A blast of fire-warmed air stung her face. Turning toward Anniston, she smiled expectantly. This was the moment she had been waiting six months for. The moment where they might start their marriage again and do their level best to love and appreciate each other in spite of their differences.

Anniston gave her a stiff smile, patted her formally on the shoulder, and pecked her cheek. There wasn't the embrace and kiss she had hoped. Then he slapped his hands together and turned toward the fire. "Let me get these logs blazing for you, dear," he said, grabbing the poker and busying himself with the fire.

Prodding and twisting the logs, he began a nervous, steady patter. "A moment here, and I'll have the fire blazing. You must be frozen. Really, Glynette, you should have spent the night in Harding," he scolded. He chucked another log on the fire, then went to work with the poker again, rearranging to his satisfaction.

She stared at his back, momentarily bewildered, but then reminded herself that it was typical of Anniston. He tended to overdo form in favor of feeling. He must have missed her during the six months apart. He had said as much in his letters, though admittedly with little passion. He would need a few minutes to settle down.

"I hope the house is to your liking," Anniston continued, giving the log a final jab and closing the stove. "I bought the furniture from Major Dixon who lived here before. He's retiring, and he and his wife have returned to Washington."

He rubbed his palms together, as though trying to start another fire between them. "I'm certain you'll like it here, my pet, in spite of the weather. The other ladies have all manner of activities to stay busy. They've been anxious for you to arrive."

Glynette, too exhausted and chilled for so much conversation, did her best to keep up as she unpinned her hat and tugged at her damp gloves. She rubbed her hands together, then grabbed at her cheeks to work some feeling into them. Each felt hot, not cold, as though a blazing iron had been pressed against the tender flesh.

The door opened again, and Gregor stepped into the parlor, setting down the last of Glynette's bags. "Pop on over whenever you like," he called on his way out. "The champagne's chilled and ready to pour."

Glynette smiled kindly at Gregor until the door closed behind him. Then she turned to Anniston with a questioning look.

"Oh, didn't Gregor tell you?" Nervously, he ran a thumb and forefinger down each side of his blond mustache. "Lucy's invited us to dinner. A little party to celebrate your arrival."

Glynette sighed, sat on the davenport, and began pulling off her boots and peeling away her damp stockings. She held an icy foot in her hands, rubbing the circulation back into it. Her hair had fallen into loose strands, her face was pale and drawn, and the lamp light showed dark circles beneath her eyes.

"Here," he said, kneeling before her. Peering anxiously into her face, he took her other foot into his hands and rubbed. "I know you're tired, Glynette, but Lucy has several guests waiting for you, including the major, and they'd be sorely disappointed if you didn't show. You're the guest of honor." He smiled beseechingly.

"What if I had stayed in Harding?"

"But you didn't."

Glynette gave a dejected sigh, halfway wishing she had stayed after all. "I had thought we might have our first evening alone," she said, reaching out to draw her fingertips along his cheek. "There's time for the others tomorrow."

A desperate feeling had chilled her, touching places the Montana cold had missed. Time had collapsed upon the two of them, she thought. Six months had not passed, after all. Nothing had changed. Here was the same Anniston—remote and calculating, an ambitious Army officer concerned foremost with appearances.

And admittedly, here was the same Glynette, wanting to live life on her own terms. The Army was the same, too, apparently, with all its political scheming, maddening parties, and petty concerns, even in so remote a place as this.

She sensed that her only hope would be to kindle a passion that could transcend their differences. Staring into Anniston's eyes, she tried to convey her desire to connect with him, to love him, and have him love her in return. But he only stroked his mustache and stared at her expectantly. The thought of loving her, of stealing even a few minutes alone with her, appeared to be as remote from his thoughts as Fort Reynolds from Washington.

Sliding forward on the davenport, she hiked her skirt above her knees and planted one foot on either side of him. She leaned forward, slid her arms across his shoulders, and pressed her lips to his. She kissed him deeply, feeling the frustrated passion of her whole soul concentrated in the kiss. Pressing against him, she willed love to flow through her, to somehow reach her husband's heart. He returned the kiss, but his lips and his body remained stiff. When at last she felt that her best effort had kindled nothing, she pulled away and smiled sadly.

Anniston looked uneasy. "We'll have many hours alone, dear," he said. "But Lucy's gone to so much trouble, and . . ."

She held up a hand, gently, to stop him. She understood the importance of social gatherings in Army life. She understood that it would be a social and political gaffe for Anniston if she failed to attend a party thrown in her honor.

"That was very kind of Lucy," she said, still wearing a wan smile. "She shouldn't have." She moved to the stove and held her stinging hands to it. "Are my clothes here?"

Anniston sighed with relief. "They arrived days ago," he said eagerly. "Look, I'll fetch your blue dress so you can change in front of the fire."

She touched her hair, wrinkled her nose, and looked down at herself. She felt coated in soot and grime. "I had thought I might have a hot bath. I haven't had one since I left Washington."

Anniston's face fell. "Everyone's waiting. It would take too long to boil the water now."

"Yes, I suppose it would," she said, irritated at him for showing less concern for her comforts than for those of others. Then she felt irritated with herself for feeling irritated at him. It was a small thing, really, and one must compromise in a marriage.

She gave a small nod to indicate that she would forgo the bath. Anniston breathed a second sigh of relief and started for the stairs. He turned at the landing and hesitated. "I had hoped you might be wearing curls about your face now."

Glynette's Corporal 17

She smoothed her fingers along the sleek, pulled-back hair at her temple. "No, I still do not care for them."

He opened his mouth to speak, then seemed to think the better of it and continued up the stairs.

Left alone, Glynette huddled before the fire. The logs hissed and crackled. Anniston's footsteps sounded overhead, squeaking a loose board. She looked around the tiny Army parlor. Though small, she knew it was elegant by Army standards. Many Army wives lived in the shacks and tents of less established forts, and she was quite fortunate not to be sitting in a two-room adobe hut with scorpions for company, the ceiling crumbling into her hair, and nothing outside but a scorching desert, rattlesnakes, and Apaches.

Anniston had been staying in bachelor officers' quarters until just a few days ago, so the house had an unlived-in look, no pictures or knickknacks. But thanks to the major's wife who had occupied it previously, a warm rosy paper decked the walls and organdy curtains hung in generous folds over the front window. The davenport, ornately carved walnut covered in a rose-patterned upholstery, was flanked by two wine-colored armchairs. A comfortable easy chair rounded out the group. It was a delightful little house, she thought—one in which a happy marriage might exist.

Tearing herself from the warmth of the fire, Glynette picked up a lamp and wandered through the rest of the house. She tiptoed gingerly from the parlor into the dining room, shadows bobbing and flickering before the advancing light. There was no fire in the dining room fireplace, and the mantel was bare, but a mahogany table filled the small space beneath a modest cut-glass chandelier, and the walls were richly clad in burgundy paper covered with climbing vines. Candles still stuck half-burned in the brass candle-holders of the chandelier, relics of a dinner party.

She stepped down the hallway into the kitchen, the light flickering dull echoes from the copper pots and iron skillets which hung from hooks on the walls. She wanted to open the cupboards and explore the servant's room at the back, but she suddenly shuddered and made a quick retreat to the parlor, stepping gingerly, for the floor was icy and the house cold away from the parlor's fire.

Shivering at the hearth, she wondered how she would ever bear the harsh winters of the eastern Montana plains. Maybe we'll be transferred to Arizona, after all, she thought. Then I'll have only sunburn and Apaches to worry about. She giggled out loud, then drew her hand to her mouth and realized she was getting punchy.

Anniston's footsteps sounded on the stairs. He entered with a quizzical smile. "What's so funny?"

"I'm just tired and giddy. I was trying to decide if I'd choose Arizona Apaches or Montana winters—if I had a choice." She smiled at him appealingly.

Anniston scowled.

He hadn't missed the note of hysteria in the outburst. He certainly hoped his wife would behave well at the party. Glynette often failed to maintain a dispassionate composure. She tended to laugh out loud, express indignation at some social injustice, or touch people in moments of excitement. Her intensity kept him on edge.

"Try to make a good impression tonight, dear. The major is an influential man. He could be important to my career."

He thrust the dress toward her. "And please don't giggle like that. It makes you sound so . . . common."

It was obvious that the party was already under way at the Britzmans' as Glynette and Anniston entered on a cold blast of wind. They could hear the parlor humming with conversation, Gregor's jovial baritone rising above the others. Lucy met them at the door, but before she could greet her guest of honor, her Pomeranian darted forth in a volley of shrill barks.

"Oh, Dolly, stop that!" Lucy shrieked before turning again to her guests. The little dog continued its vigil of circling and barking.

Lucy hugged and kissed Glynette, held her back for inspection, and said loudly, above the barking, "You're as lovely as ever, dear." She rolled her eyes at Anniston. Her voice had lost none of its grating, syrupy quality. "Of course, she would be! She hasn't been freezing out here like the rest of us." She cackled and offered to take Glynette's wrap.

Glynette smiled politely at the jab and thought to herself that Lucy Britzman—short, fleshy, round, with beady dark eyes—had not changed either. Ostentatiously gay, loud, and wielding small, invisible daggers, Lucy still put Glynette instinctively on guard.

They stepped through the foyer and entered the tiny parlor carefully. It was crowded with diminutive pieces of furniture—little chairs, pedestals, and whatnots that contrasted bizarrely to the fleshy woman who occupied it and forced visitors to constrain their movements. Straightback chairs were filled with officers in full dress uniforms and women in dinner attire. Lucy stood in the doorway scowling at Gregor and cleared her throat loudly.

The conversation stalled, then shifted to a hail of greetings and hugs directed at Glynette. These were from Gregor and the other couple she knew from Washington, Major Douglas Johnson, a career Army man in his late fifties, now the commanding officer at Fort Reynolds, and his wife Agnes. Agnes Johnson was a gentle, surprisingly unassuming woman, given her position. Not the usual

Army queen. She had kind, sparkling blue eyes, haloed by a cloud of silver hair, and a soothing voice.

"Forgive me for not having your welcoming party at the major's house," Mrs. Johnson said, grasping Glynette's hand in her own, "but this spring storm has taken the roof from our kitchen annex." She chuckled. "We're delighted you're here, nonetheless, dear child. Your beauty will refresh us after this long, dreary winter, and what a boost you will be to the men's morale!"

A round of laughter followed, and Glynette blushed. To cover her embarrassment, she lifted the glass of wine Gregor had given her and sipped, appreciating the warmth it spread throughout her chilled, tired body. She sipped nervously throughout the next hour, as she was introduced to the other guests, and they all sat about on stiff chairs, politely demanding the details of Glynette's trip west.

While Glynette spoke, Anniston stared vaguely in her direction, a taut, automatic smile on his lips. He was counting his losses. For the last six months, he had lived as a bachelor, bunking with Lieutenant Randall in bachelor officers' quarters, affectionately called Bedlam. He had not found it at all disagreeable to spend his spare time playing cards, drinking, hunting, and ice fishing in the company of other men. Now his gambling and drinking days in Bedlam were over, as were his escapades to Harding's brothels and saloons.

Draining his wine glass, he returned his attention to the conversation. Noticing the stunned admiration on the faces of the men who were seeing Glynette for the first time, he reminded himself that most men would say he had little to complain about. He chuckled inwardly. Oh, how they whinnied and pawed the ground for Glynette!

Maynard the surgeon, a strangely youthful, innocent man for the grisly job he held, looked almost worshipful, unconsciously mimicking Glynette's moves; laughing when she laughed, faintly nodding his head when she nodded hers.

Infantry Captain Frank Allen Sherry stared like a hungry dog, a lascivious light shining in his black eyes as they moved up and down the blue silk sleekly enveloping Glynette's bosom and trim waist and pooling around her hips.

Every man wanted her eyes on him and competed for her attention, for she had an intensity about her gaze that caused women to find her compassionate, and made men think she desired them. Though she had lost her appeal for him, Anniston had to concede that his wife was fetching, nevertheless. He himself had once been susceptible to her beauty.

If only she would use what charms she had to some advantage, he thought, watching her as she listened attentively to Gregor. She nodded encouragingly and smiled at some corny anecdote he told. Her slightly parted lips revealed the small, pearly teeth between them. Her pale, silky skin shone.

Unconsciously, Anniston curled his lip as she gave the lieutenant an adoring kiss on his cheek. Here was the trouble with Glynette, he mused. She had no ambition, no savvy, no wits at all that he could tell. Her first night here, and she was wasting it doting on a mediocre lieutenant at the end of his career, when she might be buttering up the major and his wife or the captains who were on their way up and could be of some use to Anniston.

When Glynette realized Anniston was staring at her, she caught his look and smiled at him quizzically. He returned the smile, raising his glass in a mock salute and turned his attention to the major's wife.

When the guests had gathered in Lucy's dining room and were crowded around the cramped white-clothed table set with silver and china and tall, slender tapers, the major's wife leaned across the table and asked Glynette, "I thought I would be the first to ask—do you ride and shoot?"

She winked at Gregor who sat at the head of the table between them. He laughed and leaned back slightly as a servant filled his glass. "Those are the two skills required to win respect on a western Army post," he said.

To the major's wife, he added, "I can tell you for a fact, Mrs. Johnson, that no woman here rides more skillfully than Mrs. McCrae."

Glynette tossed Gregor a look of mock exasperation. "I would rather not have to prove myself as 'accomplished,' and I certainly cannot shoot at all. In fact, I'm terrified of guns."

"You'll get used to them, dear," Mrs. Johnson insisted. "You must learn to shoot."

"If Anniston doesn't teach you, I will," said Gregor, giving her arm a protective pat.

From the far end of the table, Lucy called, "Mrs. McCrae?"

Forming a civil smile, Glynette turned to Lucy.

Lucy offered a bite of meat to the Pomeranian that sat on her lap, then leaned forward and said, "Tell me, dearie, who's your striker? Do you know yet?"

Glynette smiled and looked around. The whole table was listening. "My . . . *striker*?"

"Yes, you know . . . your servant, a soldier to cook, chop wood, do chores. Oh, you are new at this!" she cackled, shuttling a conspiring glance at one of the other women.

Captain Lewis' wife, Maggie, a pale, pretty woman with delicate features and large wide-set gray eyes, turned to Glynette and explained. "Enlisted men are often hired as servants, as it's almost impossible to keep a hired girl.

There are so few women, if you find one she ends up marrying one of the soldiers . . ."

"I see," Glynette said, uncertain if she liked the idea of having one of the soldiers in her house. They were typically coarse, crude men.

Anniston cleared his throat and said to Lucy, "I picked Thomas Flint, my best corporal."

"Thomas . . . ?" Glynette said, stopping her fork halfway to her mouth.

Gregor turned to her, grinning broadly. "Tom! The big soldier who lifted the wagon off the Chinaman."

"Wagon?" Major Johnson raised his brows.

Gregor told the story, turning crimson with excitement and gesturing broadly as he relished his descriptions of Tom Flint's strength and heroism.

When Gregor finished the story, Major Johnson laughed. "That young fellow's a trump."

Anniston nodded. "He's not your average yellowleg." To Glynette he added, "Just remember, he's there to follow your orders. If he gives you any trouble, I'll have him flogged"—he rolled his eyes toward the major—"or we'll shave half his head and drive him off the post to the tune of 'The Rogue's March.' "

The men laughed. Glynette felt suddenly light-headed and weary. Remembering the broad-shouldered man with the melancholy eyes filled her with an inexplicable dread. Out of the two hundred and fifty men in garrison, why did it have to be him?

Anniston leaned toward her, scowling. "Is something wrong, dear? He didn't offend you somehow, did he?"

"Oh, no!" She cleared her throat. "It's just that Mr. Flint seems like such a . . . capable . . . man. I hate to take him away from duties more worthy of his . . . strength."

Major Johnson laughed, tossed his napkin onto his empty plate, slid back his chair, and crossed his long, willowy legs. "Yes, he's a strong, strapping country boy from Tennessee," he intoned in a mock Southern twang. "A big man, too, almost too big for the cavalry, but one of our best riders, nevertheless."

Gregor listened impatiently to this description then turned to Glynette. "Tom will make an excellent servant for you," he reassured her. "He's clean, hardworking, polite, and the men say he can cook like a French chef."

This elicited a round of laughter, for certainly none of the ruffians and hayseeds who soldiered in the frontier Army had ever eaten French cuisine.

Gregor shrugged. "That's an exaggeration, perhaps, but I've tasted his griddlecakes, and they melt in your mouth." He smiled at her warmly and crossed his arms on his broad chest.

Glynette dropped her eyes and patted her lips with her napkin. For some reason, she did not want Mr. Flint as her servant. She did not want him in or around her home. There was something about the man that had touched her. It was a primal, instinctual attraction, she felt, and it appalled her. But she certainly could not voice this apprehension to the people before her now, nor could she press Anniston to find another striker without a plausible explanation.

Suddenly she realized the others were staring at her. Anniston said, "Are you all right, my dear?"

She blushed deeply. "I'm fine, just a little tired."

"Well, in that case," Lucy said, pushing the Pomeranian from her lap and smoothing the folds of her dress, "we'd better go right to dessert and coffee so you, my poor dear, can get some sleep."

For the remainder of the evening Glynette maintained a company smile but was visibly agitated. Her eyes were vacant, and she occasionally blushed for no reason. Half of her thoughts were still with the strange, big man with

Glynette's Corporal

the kind eyes who had saved the Chinaman. She shivered almost imperceptibly, inexplicably stirred.

Tom Flint was exhausted and chilled to the bone. His back ached, his eyes burned, and his curled fingers were frozen stiff around his reins, but before he could warm himself by the barracks fire and collapse onto his cot, he still had to tend the mules and horses.

Nevertheless, Tom was happy. He had not only helped bring Captain McCrae's wife safely to the fort tonight, he had also saved a man's life. As he worked, he murmured thanks for the strength that aided him, and didn't forget to extend his gratitude to the hardworking mules and horses. They'd had a hard night, too, and tired as he was, he took the time to rub them down, give them some extra oats, cover them with warm blankets, and say a few words of appreciation.

When Tom had carefully covered his own horse with a blanket against the night chill, he closed the wide stable doors and entered the back door of the cavalry barracks. He strode the length of barracks to his cot. He hung his ice-covered ratskin cap and buffalo coat on a peg and unfastened the brass buttons of his Army coat. Finally, he kicked off his heavy field boots and lay down, arms folded behind his head.

Across from him, in front of the iron box stove, several men sat on shipping crates around a scarred wooden table playing poker and smoking. A cloud of gray smoke hung in the air around their heads, glowing eerily in the light cast by the pair of oil lamps hanging from the rafters. Others sat or lay on their bunks nearby.

After a round of high stakes, the game ended when one of the gamblers cursed, slammed back his chair, and stalked away. The winner of the pot, Virgil Tell, First Sergeant of E Company, looked up at Tom with a victorious grin. "Hey, Tom, you made it. Did you deliver our new cavalry queen?"

"Yep, she's in the hands of the good captain now," Tom said, turning his head for a better look at his friend Virgil, a lanky redhead with a drooping, untrimmed mustache and kind, lake-blue eyes. Virgil also was a Southerner, as was most of Company E. Though the war had been over for more than a decade now, Army command still liked to keep the 'galvanized Yankees' lumped together.

"That's all we need, another skirt around the post. She good lookin'?"

"The purtiest woman you ever seen, Virg."

Ropey, a small red-faced man with sparkling black eyes, had left the game and now lay on his cot across from Tom's smoking a cigarette. He smiled insinuatingly in Tom's direction and said, "It's about time we had somethin' purty to look at around here. You'd think with the benefits of money and easy livin', these officers' wives might have somethin' up on the livestock." He snorted and, turning to face the wall, took a covert swig from a flask.

Virgil looked over at Tom lying on his cot. "How 'bout I deal you in, Tom? Sutton's mad again. The man just don't know how to lose gracefully." He grinned as he stacked his pennies and nickels into neat columns.

Tom shook his head without raising up from the bed. "No, thanks. It's been a long two days."

Virgil guffawed and glanced around at the others. "Now listen to that. You been in Harding for nearly two days waitin' for that train to get through, and I bet you didn't drink more'n a couple beers. You didn't do a bit o' gamblin', of course, and I'm sure none o' the girls on the line benefitted by your presence either. What're you so worn out about? Now if you'd let go of a little o' that money, Tom, I think you'd find it a mite refreshin'. Try it." He shuffled the cards and grinned.

Tom waved him off. "Lay off, Virg. I just want to lay right here and have a last snort of all you sweatin' and fartin' rednecks before I move over to the captain's quarters."

Virgil guffawed and dealt to the three men still at the table. Tim Cockburn piped in, kicking back in his chair. "You'll be missin' this sweet smell after a couple days over at the high society house. You'd best come on over of an evenin', give us a chance at some o' that extry five dollars you'll be a-earnin'."

Ropey snorted with disgust. "I can't believe you'd hire out as a striker, Tom. You ain't gonna take to kowtowing to no officer's wife. I don't care how purty she is."

Tom smiled but said nothing. He would miss them. After years of living in close quarters with these men, working and fighting by their sides, they were as good a bunch of friends as he'd ever had—and his only family. The galvanized Yankees.

Once he moved into Captain McCrae's quarters, he would no longer be one of them. They would call him "dog robber" and become suspicious of his close association with an officer. That's why he had never hired out as a striker before. But with less than three years left in the Army, he now felt a stronger pull. He needed money. The one thing he wanted even more than friendship was to buy Orsen Demmer's horse ranch in the Antelope Mountains.

Chapter Two

Glynette, awake for most of the night, had just fallen into a troubled sleep when the rafters shook with the dull boom of the reveille gun. She opened her eyes to an energetic trumpet call and the sound of someone humming along. While asleep she'd felt the unceasing swaying of the train and dreamed she was still in the Pullman. Then she saw Anniston's covers thrown back, his pillow lying rumpled and askew, and remembered where she was.

Tears of disappointment sprang to her eyes as she remembered the night before. After the party, Anniston had been irritable and cold, scolding her for her performance at the party and rejecting her attempts at wifely tenderness. It was too unfair. She had attended the party for his sake and done her best to be gracious, but whatever she did was never enough. She buried her face in her pillow, as though to blot out the memory.

She had hoped that the months apart might have softened his attitude toward her, that he might be as anxious as she for a new start, but he seemed determined to cling tenaciously to his disappointment in her. He had disappointed her in many ways, too, but she never forgot that they were obligated by their vows to honor and to love each other. She could not reconcile herself to spending her life in a sham of a marriage, could not face the dismal realization that things were at least as bad between her and Anniston as they had been before. And worse, he seemed to have no interest in improving things.

Anniston appeared in the dressing room doorway, buttoning the cuffs of his blouse. "How did you sleep?" he asked, his tone now polite and formal.

"Fine," she said, forcing herself onto her elbows.

"Catch up on your rest, dear." Anniston pulled on his wool coat and went to work on the big, brass buttons. "Tom's downstairs chopping wood. He'll fix you breakfast whenever you're ready."

"Will I see you today?"

"I'm on duty." He crossed the room with a preoccupied air, and pecked her on the cheek. "I'll see you tonight," he said, then walked out of the bedroom.

She stared after him, wondering anew at his indifference toward her. It was obvious he hadn't been lonely for her. Her arrival seemed to have made no more impression on him than an unpleasant change in the weather.

His footsteps sounded through the rooms downstairs, a door opened and slammed shut, and the house was quiet. She dropped her head to the pillow. When she woke again, bright sunlight poured into the bedroom and the rhythmic sounds of wood being split. She lay listening, dozing in and out of sleep until she heard the door to the house open and close, then the sound of logs being tumbled onto the hearth.

Opening her eyes, she knew instantly it was Tom Flint. She heard the grating sounds of the fire being stoked, another log added, the poker returned to its place. She wondered at his presence there, right beneath her. But when she considered that she would soon have to pull herself into the stature of a captain's wife and give him orders, she pulled the covers over her head and closed her eyes again.

Soon the door opened and closed, and the regular rhythm of the ax resumed. Glynette pushed back the covers, grimaced as she slipped into the travel clothes she had worn for the last six days, and went downstairs. She warmed herself by the fire, though she soon realized there was no need. Corporal Flint had stoked the parlor and kitchen fires until the whole house was balmy, and Glynette was warm for the first time in days. She felt the aching muscles that had been unconsciously clenched against the chill finally loosen and relax.

The door opened again. Glynette started, then turned resolutely to face the big soldier who had caught her admiring him yesterday.

"Mornin', Mrs. McCrae." He smiled a polite close-lipped smile, a handsome visage in a buckskin mackinaw and wool hat, chiseled cheeks ruddy from the cold. "Here's more wood for you. This cottonwood burns fast and don't put off a lot of heat, so you have to keep it piled on."

She noted the Southern accent, found it amusing, then watched silently as he added the wood to the growing heap. Then he turned, straightened his shoulders, and announced, "I'm Corporal Thomas Flint."

He removed a deerskin glove and offered his hand. Tentatively, she shook it. It was a big hand, with a lot of power concealed in the scarred fingers. But he gave Glynette's hand the slightest, gentlest squeeze. She still felt the warmth of his skin after he released her hand.

Glynette looked again into the serious green eyes and tried to keep her gaze steady. "This is a little unusual for me, Mr. Flint. I've never had a man . . ." She couldn't quite think how to finish the sentence. She stammered, silently trying out several versions, unable to give voice to any.

"Yes, ma'am, I know what you're thinkin'," Tom said, rescuing her. "But I assure you I can do any job a woman can, and I'll prove it to you right now by fixin' you some breakfast."

In fact, Glynette didn't think it odd that a man could cook or tend house. She'd spent many weekends with her wealthy friends back East who employed chefs and butlers. But those men did not cause the turmoil in her emotions that Tom Flint did. Grateful that he had misunderstood the nature of her discomfort, she nodded as though all her apprehensions had been relieved. "Well . . . I'm glad to hear that you are so capable, Mr. Flint."

"You might as well call me Tom."

He looked straight into her face with eyes so keen it seemed they could see right through her. "All right . . . Tom. And, thank you, I would love some breakfast."

He shrugged out of his coat and hung it on the rack by the door, removed his cap and smoothed a hand over his heavy, chestnut-colored hair. Then he strolled down the hallway into the kitchen annex.

"Is there anything I can do?" Glynette called after him.

"No, ma'am. You just relax . . ."

As the sounds and smells of breakfast being prepared emanated from the kitchen, Glynette sat on the davenport, her arms folded along its back, and looked out the front window. The fort looked stark in the morning light, a monotonous rectangle of white frame buildings surrounding a broad parade ground bordered by mounds of shoveled snow and desolate rows of cottonwood saplings. It appeared to her like some remote and austere Scandinavian village built around a square, in the center of which stood a high flagpole and a cannon.

"We're a ways from Washington," she muttered.

When Tom had called her to the table, and she'd taken her seat, he brought out a plate steaming with fresh biscuits, fried eggs, and two slices of dark meat.

"Quail," Tom said before she could get the question out.

"I don't believe I've ever had quail."

"It's not my favorite meat, but it's plentiful hereabouts, and at least it's a change from Army beef. I roasted this one with chokecherry jelly. Captain McCrae said it wasn't half bad."

"Then it must be wonderful," Glynette said, knowing Anniston's delicate palate.

She stole a look at Tom's face as he refilled her teacup. He was a rugged man, it was true, but in spite of the grim set of his jaw and the somber look in his eyes, he appeared gentle and dignified. He didn't seem to resent his servant position.

When he returned to the kitchen, she tore open a biscuit, butter-brown on top, a tender, fluffy cloud inside. She spread butter on the biscuit, scooped jam into the buttery nest, and took a bite. Delicious. She clearly had no reasonable objection to having Tom as her striker. He seemed a capable cook and a hard worker, as Gregor had said he would be.

While she was still considering Tom's attributes, he appeared in the doorway. "I have water on the stove for a bath, whenever you're ready." Then he disappeared.

Glynette arched a brow and sipped her tea. No reasonable objection indeed!

While Tom cleared the table and filled the copper tub in the small storage room off the kitchen, Glynette went upstairs to change. Slipping out of the gray travel suit and letting it drop in a heap, she wondered if it would ever be wearable again, soiled as it was with coal soot and travel dust. She felt like taking the whole stack, undergarments included, and throwing them on the fire. But she left them on the floor, pulled her wrapper around her, and rummaged in her trunks for a fresh dress.

As she descended the stairs, clutching her favorite soaps and oils, she felt momentarily embarrassed at having Tom see her in her dressing gown. Then she realized, hearing the steady rhythm of the ax, that the soldier had judiciously removed himself from her path.

Once inside the little makeshift washroom, she gasped with pleasure to see steam rising from a copper tub filled with hot water. She tested the water with her toes, then, finding it to her liking, stepped in. She grasped the sides of the tub and, sighing with satisfaction, slid in slowly up to her neck.

"Heavenly," she sighed.

As a cloud of lavender-scented steam enveloped her and a trickle of sweat slipped down her cheek, she gave in to the delight of the bath. The warm water caressed her, like a gentle man's loving hand, and for awhile she dozed and slipped into a happy dream.

Anniston McCrae mounted his gray gelding and exited the stables behind the main compound, returning the guard's salute as he cantered away from the fort. He loped toward the brushy river bottom behind the stables and turned west, following the river, toward an Indian camp on the post's reserve about a mile upstream.

He had spent the better part of the morning doling out assignments, listening to complaints from his noncommissioned staff, and making his reports. Now he was free to perform his daily "inspection" of the Indian camp.

As he approached the camp—a ragtag assortment of teepees, canvas huts, and one-room cabins—he scanned the dwellings and satisfied himself that all was quiet. Smoke rose in columns from the dingy, snow-banked teepees. Several women wrapped in Army-issue blankets and buffalo robes cooked around common fires, chattering and cackling. Children stumbled in the heavy snow, giggling and pelting each other with balls of ice. Thin dogs that resembled famished wolves wandered in search of stray morsels.

When Anniston reached the first teepee, a girl no older than sixteen stepped from it and cast her eyes warmly toward the approaching officer. Anniston reined his horse, dismounted, and tethered it to a nearby cottonwood. He had scarcely released the reins before the girl wrapped her arms around his neck, pressed herself against his chest, and beamed up at him expectantly. He smoothed back her hair and lowered his lips to hers. He kissed her hungrily, roughly, moving his mouth over her face, then back to her lips. "Lark," he whispered.

"I didn't know if you would come," she said, pouting. "I heard your wife had arrived."

"I'll always come," he said, chuckling. "I appreciate my allies."

"You have been with her?" The girl's eyes were accusing.

"No," he lied. "I have no need for another. Just you." Grasping her hand, he pushed aside the canvas flap of the teepee and guided her through. He felt his way past the fire that burned in the center of the lodge. In the furthest shadowed corner, they fell onto the girl's soft bed of skins.

Glynette arranged a doily on a walnut end table, set a pink cameo bowl in a silver basket in the center of it and stood back to study the effect. She stepped back further to take in the whole room. She had hung two large oval portraits of her own and Anniston's parents over the davenport. Several of her botanical studies and a wedding portrait of her and Anniston decorated the remainder of the parlor's walls.

That looks more like a home, she thought. Just then the bugler sounded the call for afternoon fatigue. Glancing at the clock on the mantel, she wrinkled her nose. "Duty calls."

An hour later, she sat in Maggie Lewis' parlor with seven other officers' wives, balancing a teacup and saucer in one hand and nibbling a tea cake with the other. She was bored. For the last hour, the women had complained about the difficulty of keeping up with the latest fashions while living in Montana, and had insisted that Glynette describe the new spring styles in detail.

The women chattered and competed in high voices, constantly interrupting each other. They assailed each other with subtle insinuations, probed their enemies for weaknesses, and exchanged covert glances with their allies. Glynette was amazed to find such a tea party— petty and droll enough to challenge any in Washington— in this most uncivilized part of the West.

The women sported newly sewn but outdated spring dresses, abundantly trimmed with ribbons, ruffles, and tassels, and new spring bonnets covered with tea roses, poppies, and giant satin bows. A stuffed parrot perched atop Dinah Sherry's hat in a nest of pink ostrich plumes.

Glynette heard her name and returned her attention to the conversation. "Well, you're the smart one, Mrs. McCrae," Betsy Evans, a plump blond, was saying as she buttered her third scone, "staying in Washington for the winter."

Several others nodded in agreement. "Absolutely," said Sibyl Nye, her pinched brown eyes separated by two deep frown lines. "That was the sensible thing for you. Unfortunately, I'm Army through and through. I have to be with the regiment." She laughed with feigned self-deprecation.

"Likewise," concurred Dinah Sherry in a heavily-exaggerated Kentucky accent.

Glynette sensed that all the women, having spent the winter with the Army, shared Sibyl's smugness. They assumed she had stayed in Washington for the sake of her own comfort. If she explained that no amount of arguing or pleading would persuade Anniston to bring her to Montana with him last fall, they would assume she was making excuses.

She smiled. "I certainly admire all of you for enduring the winter here. If *April* is like this, I can't imagine what you must have suffered in the winter months."

The women murmured a chorus of agreement.

A sudden loud cry issued from the back room. "Excuse me, ladies," Maggie said, setting down the teapot, "Neddie's awake and is issuing orders for lunch."

After Maggie left, Lucy said, "It was a brutal winter, but I'm glad I was here with Lieutenant Britzman."

"Oh, Lucy," Sibyl scoffed, "this winter was nothing—there was no real hardship." To Glynette she added, "I've been in the far West for ten years and have seen much worse conditions."

Lucy spread her lips into a sneer and rolled her eyes at Glynette. With exaggerated politeness, she said, "As I recall, Mrs. Nye, you spent six of those years at Angel Island. Or was it the Presidio? Not exactly wilderness conditions." She chuckled and glanced around the group, eliciting a few supportive laughs.

Sibyl smiled acidly. "Admittedly, my husband has been rewarded with some comfortable posts for his ability. It was by his own choice that he came to Montana... unlike some others."

The room went quiet. Lucy's face reddened. The women all knew that Lucy felt that Gregor, who had made his way up through the ranks the hard way, had often been snubbed by Army command because he wasn't a West Point man. For Sibyl to suggest that her own husband had been rewarded for talent rather than pedigree was a slap.

"Mrs. Nye," Lucy hissed, her massive bosom heaving.

Carrying baby Ned on her hip, Maggie entered the parlor and froze, her eyes on Lucy. With the instincts of a fine Army hostess, she immediately sensed the threat to the success of her tea party. With her free hand she plucked a silver tray covered with white cakes from the sideboard.

"Lucy," she blurted, thrusting the cakes under Lucy's nose. "You simply must try one of these. It's a new recipe."

Lucy gave Maggie a dangerous look, then smiled acidly, took one of the cakes, and passed the plate. As the tray made its way around the circle, the women nibbled, loudly exclaiming their approval, and begged for the new recipe. But Maggie's diversion had clearly not arrested the duel. Lucy's eyes were nearly crossed with fury, and when the chitchat about the cakes finally stalled, she drew in another breath to retaliate against Sibyl Nye.

This time Lila Carter, the fifteen-year-old child bride of Lieutenant Manfred Carter, jumped in before Lucy could speak. "Mrs. McCrae, I must ask, how did you endure being apart from Captain McCrae all winter?" She unconsciously twisted her wedding ring. "I can't bear to be away from Manny even overnight."

Glynette forced another ingratiating smile. "It was difficult, of course, dear—but honestly, it was Anniston who insisted I remain in Washington." She cast a guilty look around the circle of women. "Really, I hated not being here for him."

Maggie Lewis caught her eye and gave her a sympathetic, slightly amused smile. Glynette, surprised and grateful, returned the smile, but Maggie's attention had already turned to Ned, who had suddenly grown tired of waiting for his lunch and let out a plaintive wail.

Maggie, shushing the baby and glancing nervously at Lucy, could only hope that the disaster had been averted. She invited everyone to help themselves to more tea and cakes, and disappeared into the kitchen.

Lucy abruptly turned to Glynette, an insinuating smile curling her lips. She seemed suddenly to have forgotten her fury at Sibyl. "You needn't have worried about Captain McCrae's loneliness, my dear," she said with an air of significance.

"Oh?" Glynette stiffened. She recognized the sweetly acerbic tone.

"No, dear, he was quite busy all winter," Lucy said, glancing at Dinah, who dropped her eyes and smiled, "taking such a personal interest in the Indians, making sure their ... needs ... were met.

"I see." Glynette was thoroughly baffled. This did not sound at all like Anniston. He had always detested Indians, considering them to be little more than savage, dangerous children, incapable of reason. Further, Glynette had the distinct impression that Lucy had just flung one of her invisible daggers.

"Well," Glynette said, with a shrug, "I'm glad to hear that Anniston made it through the winter so well without me."

The women tittered, as they had given the least provocation all afternoon. Lucy and Dinah shared a conspiratorial look, and Glynette quickly looked away. Her head hurt. The miserable combination of boredom, tense laughter, and verbal fencing had taken its toll. Suddenly she felt exhausted and unbearably lonely, and could hardly wait to escape.

Long after the party had ended, the women continued to linger in Maggie's doorway, drifting from the foyer onto the veranda, chatting and making plans for upcoming parties and balls. Slowly, by ones and twos, they made their way down the steps, calling their good-byes, and meandering to their homes up and down the row of officers' quarters.

When at last she could, Glynette hurried to her house at the end of the row, the prairie wind whipping her skirts around her legs, threatening to take her hat, and rattling the flag halyards violently against their pole.

Inside, she flung herself on the davenport and unpinned her hat, tossing it onto a chair. Then she lay back and groaned. She tried to laugh, conjuring up images of the absurd Lucy Britzman and her wounded pride, Dinah Sherry with her exaggerated Southern accent, and the simpering child bride Lila Carter. But there was no one to laugh with. She had no allies here.

Her thoughts turned gloomily to the life ahead of her, to the next tea party. How would she endure it? A life of tea parties with simple-minded, mean-spirited women in this tiny, miserable, isolated fort. No family or friends. No libraries, lectures, museums, or concerts. A virtual desert surrounding her.

"A loveless marriage," she said aloud. She stared at the shadows and listened to the sound of her voice, saying what she hadn't admitted before. Her thoughts about her marriage had always been a tangled snarl of rationalizations, hopes, denials, and prayers. Now suddenly the simple truth had popped out. Anniston didn't love her. He never would. Her six-month fantasy about a new beginning with Anniston now seemed absurd. She was alone in an alien world.

Afternoon grew into late afternoon. The sunlight mellowed and shadows lengthened. Glynette stared into the gauzy light, shimmering with a mesmerizing radiance off the woven red fabric of a chair. Each thread, each raised fleur de lis caught the light with glittering clarity. Sun motes drifted quietly in the air. The sun lowered and shifted, scattering the shadows from the far corner of the room, and still Glynette lay on the davenport.

Three sharp raps on the door startled her. She sat up quickly, smoothed a hand over her hair, and looked around. She rose, smoothed her dress, and opened the door. Tom Flint stood before her, shoulders back, natty forage cap held in his hands before him.

"Afternoon, Mrs. McCrae."

She looked at him blankly a moment, then stepped back for him to enter.

"I had afternoon fatigue and stables at four, but now I'm available to take care of anything you need before I get supper for you and the captain." He smiled. Then the smile faded. He glanced about the foyer and looked back at her uncertainly.

When she looked up her face was pale, the expression in her eyes strange. She still hadn't spoken. She closed the door and remained facing it for a long moment before turning back toward the parlor, eyes down.

Wondering if he had offended her, he said, "From now on I'll let myself in the back door, but I thought since today was the first day, I'd come in the front and let you know I was here. I'll be sleepin' in the servant's room off the kitchen now . . ."

He cleared his throat and moved away from the door, watching her and sidestepping slowly down the hall toward the kitchen. "Well, I'll just . . ."

He hesitated, stopped, and looked at her closely. She stood just inside the parlor, staring at the floor. Her eyes seemed vacant, and in fact, they saw nothing, for they had suddenly become suffused with tears. He said quietly, "Could I bring you . . . some tea . . . Mrs. McCrae?"

He squinted his eyes and tilted his head toward her. "Or anything?"

She smiled a little. Then the smile twisted and her face twitched. She fought for control, but his gentle concern had erupted a well of emotion she couldn't suppress. Tears spilled onto her cheeks. She said breathlessly, "No, thank you, Tom. I've been drinking tea all afternoon."

She laughed, drew in her breath sharply and wiped her cheeks with both hands. She put her hands over her face.

"Mrs. McCrae . . ." Tom stepped forward hesitantly and took her arm. "Why don't you sit down." She dropped her hands and let him guide her back to the davenport. After she was seated, he released her arm and handed her his handkerchief. She blew her nose, put one hand over her face and turned away from him.

"Obviously, you're not feeling well, ma'am. Is there something I can do?"

She gave her head a quick shake. "No, thank you, Tom. You're very kind." She dropped her hand, looked up and tried to smile. "Really, I'm fine. I'm just silly . . . and tired, I guess." She lifted her chin toward the kitchen. "Go ahead."

"Maybe I could bring you a glass of sherry?"

"Yes . . . a glass of sherry."

When he'd left the room, Glynette cringed. Why did she have to make a fool of herself? She pounded her forehead with her fist. "You're a silly ass, Glynette McCrae."

But the shame was fleeting. Her thoughts were too painful, and soon her previous desolation had enveloped her again. When Tom returned, she sat quietly, staring without expression at a wavering patch of light on the floor. He approached her slowly and handed her the glass. "Can I do anything else for you, Mrs. McCrae?" he said softly.

She laughed, and to his dismay, tears sprang into her eyes again. "You can stop being so kind, Tom." She laughed again, and a tear streaked down her cheek. "I don't know what it is, but the way you speak to me makes me cry."

He hesitated, then laughed with her.

God, she was beautiful, he thought. The way she looked away and then looked back into his eyes before she spoke, as though she were afraid her words might cause pain. It perplexed him to see such a beautiful, gentle woman suffer, but as an enlisted man he did not presume to ask the cause of her unhappiness. He wished he could put his arms around her and comfort her.

Glynette wiped the corners of her eyes, stared at the amber liquid in her glass, and said, "Since you've seen me cry, and I've already been so silly in front of you, I might as well tell you that I'm feeling a little lonely today."

Tom nodded but didn't know what to say. The woman had just been reunited with her husband. She was beautiful. Why was she lonely? Why would a woman like her ever be lonely? Where was Captain McCrae? He looked around the room as if he expected the man to be summoned by his question. Why hadn't the captain requested leave for the day—the whole week—to be with her?

His jaw tightened, and his eyes glittered. He knew why. Most everyone at the fort knew why. He was down at the Indian camp, while his lovely wife, looking very lost and out of place, sat alone.

"I reckon you're homesick," he said gently. "Fort Reynolds is a bit different from Washington."

One corner of her mouth tilted ironically, and she seemed to lift slightly from her trance. "That's true," she said, nodding. "In many ways Fort Reynolds is different from Washington." She looked up at him, her eyes shimmering with tears. "But in most ways, it's just the same old thing."

The sorrowful evening sounds of tattoo mingled with a high-pitched wail through the duplex wall. Lucy's dog, as well as every other dog on the fort, howled at the sound of the bugle. When the cacophony had stopped, Glynette reached beside her chair to pull a small gold scissors from a basket.

As she snipped away stray threads on the back of her needlework, she heard the boards of the veranda creak and snap under a quick bounding footstep. The gong bell in the hall clanged loudly.

Anniston lowered his book and glanced at the clock. "Who do you suppose?"

Glynette shrugged resignedly and put away her sewing as he went to open the door. After-dinner visitors, she supposed. She had hoped to sit quietly by the fire this evening with Anniston. There was at least some intimacy in that, and she was feeling desperately lonely and displaced. On occasional quiet evenings in Washington, she had felt almost close to Anniston, sitting by the fire, sharing bits of news from the day. At such times their marriage seemed nearly a true union. From the hallway, she heard Anniston say jovially, "Well, well, Captain Jim Lewis. Come in, come in. To what do we owe the honor of this distinguished visit?"

After the captain had stepped into the tiny foyer, Anniston shut the door behind him with a little laugh and rubbed his hands together. Jim Lewis was a drinking and gambling man if there ever was one, and Anniston assumed Jim had come to rescue him from domestic torpor to join the nightly game of poker in the back room at the post trader's.

Jim sighed and removed his hat. He was a stocky, sandy-haired man with a round, boyish face, but tonight he looked tense and tired. "Actually, Anniston, I came to see your wife. Maggie's having another spell, and she asked if I'd fetch Mrs. McCrae to sit with her."

Anniston's smile drooped. "Sorry to hear that, Jim." He put his hand on Jim's shoulder and gently pushed him toward the parlor.

"Glynette, you remember Captain Lewis from last night?"

Glynette offered her hand. "Of course, and Mrs. Lewis was so kind to have me to tea today."

Jim took her hand and smiled apologetically. "Maggie asked if I'd fetch you." He added hurriedly, "If you'd rather not, that's all right. I told her it wasn't fair of her to bother you when you've just arrived, but sometimes when she's having one of her spells she doesn't think clearly. The paregoric she takes—"

"Spells?" Glynette asked.

"Since Ned was born, she can't seem to snap back. She has these spells. She had rheumatic fever as a child and has always been sickly. The doctor warned her not to have any more children after Helen, but . . ." He blushed and stared at the floor.

Glynette wrinkled her brow, remembering Maggie bouncing around the parlor laughing and serving tea with Ned on her hip. "She seemed fine today."

Jim spread his hands, exasperated. "That's why she's ill. Every time she starts to feel stronger, she pulls some fool stunt." He shook his head with an air of resignation. "She thought she had to take her turn at tea."

"I'll get my wrap," Glynette said. She stepped into the foyer and lifted a heavy hooded cloak from the rack. She couldn't get her mind around what was happening. She had only met Maggie Lewis today. Didn't the woman have friends to call on? Why would she send for her? As Jim had suggested, she must not be thinking clearly. Perhaps she had even already forgotten she had sent for Glynette. Most likely she would not even be lucid by the time Glynette arrived.

As she stepped down the slushy walk holding Jim's arm, Glynette was so preoccupied that she only half noticed that the wind had blown warm air in, and puddles of water had formed from the melting snow. With her free hand she held her skirts up and stepped lightly on the balls of her feet between puddles.

The sounds of a banjo and a man singing drifted from the cavalry barracks. Laughter erupted when the song ended, irritating Glynette who was troubled by this new circumstance. It had been one thing after another since she had arrived at the fort, and she had seen little of her husband.

Inside the Lewis' quarters, Jim picked up a lamp from the foyer table and led Glynette upstairs. At the top of the stairs, he pushed open the bedroom door. "Maggie," he said softly toward the mound of quilts on the bed.

When he received no answer, Glynette stepped in and whispered, "It's all right, Captain. Let her sleep. I'll just sit with her until she awakens."

A look of relief spread over the man's face as he quickly thanked Glynette and closed the door behind him, leaving Glynette alone. A fire crackled softly, but the room was otherwise quiet. The rosy dress Maggie had worn earlier lay in a limp heap across a settee in front of the fire.

Glynette took a tentative step toward the mounded bundle of quilts on the bed. Only Maggie's pale face and the top of her auburn hair poked out from the mountain of quilts, catching the yellow glow from the bedside lamp.

Far from those of the animated hostess who had served tea earlier, her eyes were sunken and shrouded in dark circles, her face gaunt. Glynette recognized the delicate features of one who had spent a long time in a childhood sickbed. Her heart swelled with pity.

Glynette sat on the straightback chair beside the bed. Nervously, she looked around the room—an exact duplicate of Anniston and hers, but without Mrs. Dixon's expensive touches. The room was plain in the Western style, the pale walls decorated only with Navajo rugs, the furniture rustic, the floor carpeted with a buffalo robe. Reluctantly, Glynette shuttled her gaze back to Maggie and was startled to see her eyes open, small and bright in their deep sockets, like a mouse's peering from a hole.

"Glynette." Maggie smiled and stirred under the covers. "Thank you for coming." She pulled a hand from underneath the covers and reached forward, groping.

Glynette took her hand, heartened by the familiar greeting. She hoped her voice did not betray her discomfort. "I was glad to do it, Maggie. Can I get you anything?"

"No, no, I just want you to sit and talk to me." She pulled her hand back in under the covers and rolled onto her side so she could see Glynette better.

"You must think it strange that I called for you."

Glynette smiled, unsure what to say.

"Jim didn't want to trouble you, but I just knew you'd understand."

"Of course," Glynette replied, wanting to reassure her, though in fact she didn't understand at all. "Why doesn't Jim stay with you?"

Maggie chuffed. "He usually does, but he's no nursemaid. He has his poker game in the evening."

Glynette regarded Maggie with renewed pity and tried to imagine herself in the same situation. She wondered how Anniston would treat her if she fell ill. "I'm glad you felt you could call on me, Maggie," she said sincerely. "The children—"

"In their room. On nights when I'm tired, the girls read or play quietly. They understand that Mama isn't well." She smiled weakly. "Ned isn't quite old enough to understand yet, but the girls do their best to keep him occupied."

Glynette regarded the array of vials and glasses on the bedside table, the shade of the lamp adjusted to protect Maggie's eyes from the light. "Are you sick all the time?"

Maggie sighed. "You saw me today. Sometimes I'm quite strong. But those days are quickly becoming fewer. I thought I'd best take my turn at tea while I still can."

Glynette understood and didn't at the same time. "Maggie . . ."

Maggie laughed bitterly. "That's right—I'm dying." She coughed, twisting her head on the pillow.

Glynette reached forward to stroke Maggie's hair until she was quiet. Her thoughts were in turmoil. Earlier that day she had envied Maggie for being the ideal officer's wife and mother. Everything Anniston wanted Glynette to be. Now she felt ashamed of her own self-pity.

Maggie turned her head toward the table. "Would you fill the spoon with some of the medicine from the blue bottle?"

As Glynette unstopped the bottle, she could see from the writing on the label that it contained paregoric. She carefully fed the medicine to Maggie, who then closed her eyes and sank heavily against the pillow.

"Thank you," she sighed. "I'll probably end up addicted to this vile liquid, but by that time it won't matter."

"Do you know how long?"

"A few weeks, months, maybe. What's the difference really? Maynard, the surgeon—you met him at dinner—says there's nothing he can do for me. I haven't told Jim."

She gasped in a breath between each sentence. "I don't think he's ready to hear it."

"You should go back East where you can be treated."

"There's nothing to be done."

"What about the children?"

"I've written my sister to ask her and her husband to take Ned. The girls will have to go to boarding school."

Glynette impulsively put her fingers to Maggie's cheek. "I'm so sorry, Maggie."

As she touched the pale, almost childish face, smoothed out by illness into a waxy mask, Glynette saw how dim the light looked in Maggie's eyes.

"Don't look so frightened, Glynette," Maggie said. "I'll be better in the morning. I just get . . . tired out." She closed her eyes. "Tomorrow I'll be fine."

Maggie appeared to have fallen asleep, but a moment later she said, "I sent for you because I thought you seemed lonely. I thought maybe you could use a friend too." She opened her eyes and stared directly at Glynette. "There's nothing lonelier than dying."

The look in Maggie's eyes was so grievous that Glynette had to force herself not to turn away.

"I don't think anyone suspects yet that my illness is getting worse," Maggie whispered. "I don't want a lot of pity. That's another reason I sent for you, Glynette. You strike me as someone who can keep a secret."

When Glynette came downstairs the next morning, she found the parlor fire blazing and the aroma of coffee and hot food emanating from the kitchen. She pulled back the drapes and looked out at the puddled parade just as the bugler stepped from the adjutant's office to sound the call for first fatigue. Dolly and the other garrison dogs raised their voices in a chorus of howls. Through the thin walls, she heard Lucy shriek, "Dolly, stop that!"

Glynette smiled. Drawing in a healthy breath she realized that she felt much stronger today. Learning of Maggie Lewis' illness had put her own petty problems in perspective. If Maggie could face her own impending death with such equanimity, then she could find a way to face her own loneliness and fear. Maggie's courage had inspired her, and the whole aspect of her new life had changed with Maggie's friendship.

She felt eager to get out into the sunshine. While the morning was still fresh, she walked around the quadrangle. She passed a sloe-eyed Indian with waist-length gray braids, his brown face as shriveled as a dried apple. "What a strangely inhabited village," she marveled to herself. Up and down the boardwalk strode blue-clad soldiers and blanketed Indians, gallant officers, young mothers pushing strollers, and pairs of ladies on morning promenades.

At the far end of the quadrangle, she entered the post trader's store, where several boisterous soldiers ordered hunks of cheese and dried fruit and devoured them on the spot. Two Indian women were bartering baskets of quilled moccasins and pelts for calico and ribbons, the mingled odors of sweat, grease, and smoke clinging to their filthy deerskins. Glynette gave them each a penny and watched with pleasure as their faces lit up.

She examined the store's cases and looked in every cubby hole, surprised by the variety of things that could be bought—every necessity and many delicacies, if one was willing to pay exorbitant prices to have them. Women's dress gloves, jewelry, perfume, and silk were sold alongside Winchester rifles, saddles, Bowie knives, and Havana cigars. Stacks of canned goods, housewares, and tools reached to the ceiling.

By the time she walked back up officers' row—carrying an overpriced sachet for Maggie, a can of oysters for Anniston, and some thread for herself—the morning guard mount had begun. She joined a group which had gathered to watch the ceremony, hear the band, and bask in the spring sunshine.

She spent the afternoon with Maggie and her daughters. They sewed and chatted and played with little Ned. It was nearly retreat when she finally went home, humming the jaunty refrain of a military tune, surprised by her relative happiness.

When Tom heard the front door open and close, he left off chopping potatoes for a stew, and took several long strides up the hallway and through the dining room. He peered through the parlor portico at Glynette and cleared his throat to let her know he was there.

When she turned, he grinned, eyes locked onto hers, not saying a word. Glynette stared at him, surprised. He had looked so solemn before. She tilted her head quizzically and said, "Well, don't you look like the cat that got the mouse."

He tilted his head in the same direction and said, "Guess again."

"What?"

"I've got a present for you. Four legs, but it's not a mouse." He folded his arms across his broad chest.

"A gift with four legs! A gift . . ."—she winced—". . . so I can't refuse it?"

He pretended to be offended, dropping his jaw and placing a hand over his heart. "Well, no, ma'am. I may be a poor plebe of a soldier, but I've got feelings too."

"Well, thank heavens it's not a mouse, anyway." She pressed her lips together. "Okay, what is it?"

"Guess."

"Tom!"

"Okay, okay, you'd never guess anyway. You probably think it's a mere dog or cat, huh?"

"That's naturally what comes to mind—you're starting to worry me."

He held up a reassuring hand. "Don't worry. It ain't a four-legged snake or whatever you're thinkin'. It's somethin' cute and fuzzy like you'd expect."

"Tom! What is it?"

"Wait right there." He disappeared down the hallway. Glynette turned back to the fire, shaking with laughter.

Tom reappeared in the doorway, his hands behind his back. "Ready?"

"As ready as I'll ever be."

"Close your eyes."

"Oh, please."

"You have to close your eyes," he insisted. "Trust me."

She closed her eyes. At least whatever the thing was, it was apparently small enough to hide behind his back. But that would include frogs and turtles and lizards. She shuddered.

"Now, hold your hands up, like you were going to hold a baby."

She held her arms up, wrists crossed, one hand under her elbow, forming a cradle. She felt him step toward her and gently place something warm and furry and squirming in her arms. Instinctively, she clutched it and opened her eyes. She gasped. Two shiny, almond-shaped black eyes stared up at her from a little squirrel-like face.

"Oh, you adorable little fellow!"

"That's a prairie dog. I don't reckon you've ever seen one."

"No, I don't suppose I have," she admitted, matching the prairie dog's look of wide-eyed amazement. "But he looks like a groundhog, if you ask me." She stroked the stiff, brown fur along its back and admired his long, pink toes. He sniffed and nibbled at the sleeve of her dress, whiskers twitching.

"A groundhog! Poor Kola." Tom reached over to stroke the insulted creature's head.

"Is Kola his name?" Her attention was drawn to Tom's tanned, weathered hand. His shirt sleeve was rolled back so she could see his broad forearm covered lightly with reddish hair. It brushed against her hand and caused her stomach to tighten.

"Now it is. I named him Kola for you. It means 'friend' in Sioux." He smiled at her, a trace of pity in his look. "I thought you could use a friend at Fort Reynolds."

She smiled up at him, then looked away and, to her dismay, her eyes filled with tears.

Thomas looked crestfallen. "Oh, no, not again! Mrs. McCrae, I . . ."

Glynette blinked quickly and gave a quick shake of her head. "No, it's all right. I'm sorry. I'm just so emotional lately, all I do is cry, and this . . ."—she looked down at the fuzzy brown creature affectionately—". . . this is very sweet. And you're right. I do need a friend."

They stared at each other a luxurious moment before she broke her gaze away. "You know, Tom," she said, "I hate to nitpick, but I do believe that Kola, though not a mouse, is nevertheless a member of the rodent family."

She held him up, peered into his face, and turned him toward Tom to have a look.

"She's got a harsh tongue," he said, giving Kola's chin a sympathetic chuck, "but I'll bet she's generous with the ginger snaps and sugar cakes."

"That I could be. I don't know a thing about how to take care of him."

"Don't worry. I'll help. He's been staying in a box, but now that spring's here, he might want to burrow himself a hole in the yard. He's gettin' pretty much grown now."

"Did you trap him?" She hated to think of the little thing being stolen from his mother.

"An Indian friend gave him to me. I shared some of my bacon and hardtack with him during the winter, and this was his way of sayin' thanks." He smiled ironically.

Glynette planted a kiss on Kola's head. "My mother was terrified when I left for Montana. She was sure that Indians or wolves would get her little girl. I can't wait to write her about my encounter with this dangerous beast."

Tom laughed. "I'll bet she sends for you straight away."

Tom had gone to the post trader's for supplies, and Glynette had settled on the couch with her new pet when she heard boots pound on the porch and the front door open and slam closed. Anniston appeared before her in full dress uniform, with his yellow-plumed helmet and white leather gloves. He was crimson with fury. "It's nearly retreat, and I've spilled coffee on my new shirt!" he yelled. "Where's the striker?"

"He just went to the post trader's," Glynette said, feeling every muscle in her body clench at her husband's unexpected appearance. No one could sour a perfectly good mood like Anniston could. "He'll be right back. Why don't you change your shirt, and . . ."

Her voice trailed off as she watched Anniston move toward her across the room, frowning, a mixture of curiosity and revulsion in his eyes. "What is . . . *that*?" He gestured at Kola.

Glynette smiled. "His name's Kola. He's a present from—"

Before she could complete the sentence, Anniston grabbed the prairie dog from her arms and turned to the kitchen, holding it by the scruff of its neck, loathing to touch it with his white dress gloves. "Good God, Glynette. It's a rat!"

"Oh, Anniston—*no, please*—Tom gave him to me!"

"But it's a rat!"

Glynette bounded up from the couch to save the squirming Kola, but she'd only made it to the kitchen when she saw the back door open and Anniston sling him into the yard. "No!" Glynette cried.

"It's a bloody rat!" Anniston yelled at her, as she ran past him and out the door.

Glynette didn't hear the door slam behind her. "Kola, Kola," she called, eyes scouring the lawn.

A gold streak caught her eye. It was Kola, running wildly and chirping like a frightened chick, probably searching for a hole.

"Oh, please come back," Glynette begged. She did not want to tell Tom that she'd already lost his present to her. Focused as she was on retrieving the frightened prairie dog, she didn't wonder why making her striker happy seemed more important at the moment than doing the same for her husband.

She'd walked for several minutes, her head turning from side to side as she scoured the grass behind the houses, when suddenly she saw the prairie dog standing before a shed on its hind legs, wringing its paws together as if in deep consternation. Its head was tipped back and sideways, its pebble-sized black eyes regarding Glynette askance.

"Oh, there you are." She moved slowly, bending over and holding out her hand in a gesture of acquiescence. "I'm so sorry, I'll never let the bad man do that to you again. Please come to me."

"What's the matter?"

Glynette turned. It was Tom, on his way back from the post trader's. He was carrying two small paper sacks.

"Kola," Glynette said mournfully. "Anniston came home and . . . he got away."

"Here." He dipped his hand into one of the sacks and offered Glynette a sugar snap. "Show him this."

Glynette took the sugar snap and held it toward the prairie dog. Kola's head flicked to the side, its tiny nose working furiously. He went down on all fours and took several steps toward Glynette before stopping and rising again on its hind legs, wringing its front paws together warily.

"Come, Kola. Take it. You like sugar snaps don't you?"

Kola lowered to all fours again and moved toward Glynette, slowly, wagging his nose and jerking his head at all the subtle noises around the fort—the voices of soldiers across the parade, the scrape of an opening window, the rustle of the breeze in the grass.

"Come on. Here you go . . ."

Finally, Kola's nose touched the sugar snap. A second later, the cookie was in his mouth, and the prairie dog was safely again in Glynette's folded arms. Not seeming to mind, it reclined there, contentedly nibbling the sugar snap it held in its paws.

Tom chuckled. "Always a sucker for a cookie."

"I'm so sorry, little one," Glynette cooed, running her cheek over the furry creature's plump body.

Tentatively, Tom said, "I hope I didn't cause any trouble between you and the captain. I can take him back to barracks if you think it best."

Glynette regarded him seriously. "Never!"

Then she stalked back to the house, Kola in her arms.

Chapter Three

One particularly warm, sunny morning in early May, Glynette sat on the davenport, lingering over an after-breakfast cup of tea and wishing she could escape her afternoon obligations.

She could see glimpses of wild flowers in the billowing grass beyond the fort and the still-tender green of the cottonwoods and willows along the river. If she were in Washington on a day like today, she thought, she would lie on a quilt in the garden with a book, dig in the flower beds, or paint a study of a robin's nest.

Since her arrival at Fort Reynolds, her afternoons had been a constant round of quilting bees, committees, and tea parties. She'd found it impossible to escape the steady stream of callers and invitations, and the obligation to return calls and extend invitations of her own. In Washington she might simply send her regrets, claim a prior engagement, or feign a headache, but in this circumscribed community, everyone knew what you were doing at every moment.

Besides feeling stifled by the fort's social structure, Glynette felt she was a virtual prisoner inside its walls.

Glynette's Corporal

She longed to wander the open prairie or venture down to the river, but Anniston had forbidden her to leave the fort without an escort. The precaution was not necessarily unreasonable, but since an escort defeated the purpose of a solitary jaunt, she had elected to spend her days thus far inside the fort.

She sighed and set her cup on the table next to her. Tom appeared in the doorway drying his hands on a towel. "What's on the agenda this afternoon?" He looked amused, as he often did, without smiling.

"Tea with the ladies. What else?"

"That's a waste of a beautiful day. You should get yourself dressed for riding."

"Don't tease, Tom. You make me feel worse."

"I'm serious. We're gettin' out of Fort Reynolds."

She laughed. "You mean we're going to make a run for it? What do they call that? A French leave?"

"No, ma'am. I'm not taking you on a French leave. This is all on the up and up. They won't send the scouts after us or put us in irons."

"Where are we going?"

"For a ride along the river. Wherever you like."

Her eyes widened as she imagined it. "You're serious?"

"Absolutely."

She frowned and looked away. "I'll have to ask Anniston." The absurdity of her own words struck her, but the fact remained, she had to have Anniston's permission if she wanted to avoid a row.

"It's all set with Captain McCrae. It was his idea, in fact. He knew you'd been wanting to get away from the post. It's not as if you kept it a secret."

"What about your fatigue duties?"

"It's on the roster, ma'am. I'm assigned to take you riding . . . if you're willing to be escorted by a mere corporal."

She could hardly suppress a whoop. "Tom, you're a

wonder. I'll get into my riding clothes." She lifted her skirt and hurried up the stairs.

Glynette was waiting on the porch when Tom rode up from the stables on a chestnut-colored gelding. He was leading the black he had ridden the day she'd first seen him in Harding. The black was fitted with a side-saddle. Tom's shaggy collie trotted alongside.

Lifting the long skirts of her riding habit, Glynette stepped off the porch as he reined up. "You're letting me ride your horse?"

"He's the only one used to a side-saddle. He's not mine, anyway. He's one of Mr. Demmer's, and he's for sale, by the way."

"For sale, huh?" Glynette studied the horse with renewed interest, smoothing her hand along its neck. "He's a beauty. But if he wants to be my horse, he'd better know how to behave himself."

"He's first-rate, Mrs. McCrae," Tom said, dismounting. "You won't find any better around here." He thought how beautiful she would look on the horse, her jet hair matching the black's silky mane.

Dan sidled up to Glynette, truckling, and she knelt to scratch him behind the ear. The grateful collie jumped up, planted a paw on each of her shoulders, and slathered her face.

"Dan, you fool," Tom admonished, pushing the dog away.

She stood and wiped her face with the back of her sleeve. "Friendly, isn't he?"

"Yeah, fine manners too," he said, scowling at Dan as he gave Glynette a hand onto the horse.

"You have to stay, Dan," Tom said firmly as he handed Glynette her reins. "Stay."

"Can't he go with us?" she asked, looking at the dog's pleading eyes.

"He belongs here." Tom chuckled. Though the stable dog officially belonged to no one, he had always favored Tom, who paid him special attention, treating him to choice game scraps from the time he was a pup. "He doesn't seem to realize his job is to guard the stables."

"Sorry, Dan," Glynette said, turning her horse. She clucked him toward the main gate. She had a light hand with the rein and the black sensed her confidence. Tom mounted, turned his horse, and fell in beside her. The collie watched them dejectedly until they were out of sight, then turned and trotted toward the stables.

"You handle that horse right well, Mrs. McCrae."

"Thanks to my father. Now if I only knew how to shoot. Everyone asks, 'Do you ride?' and 'Do you shoot?' I must say, I did not have to prove myself in those areas back East."

"Don't worry, Mrs. McCrae. You've mastered the hard part. Shootin' is easy."

The sentry waved as they passed through the gates of the compound. Out in the open, they stopped, and Glynette marveled at the distance before her. She could see for miles in the light, bright air. From the high table on which they sat, a vast prairie of swaying golden grass dipped away in every direction, rippling like ocean waves. The sky, a deep cloudless blue, hung low against the horizon. She felt engulfed by the boundless dome.

She turned to look back at the fort, sprawling amid a few scattered juneberry and buffalo berry thickets, amazed that she had lived inside it for this long now without having seen it from without. It was dwarfed by the immense prairie surrounding it. The Kettle River snaked along the back of officers' row, around the hospital and headquarters at the end of the quadrangle, then meandered across the plain toward the Indian camps.

"Would you like to ride along the Kettle?" Tom looked toward the river, swollen with the spring melt-off and shrouded with the vibrant green of newly leafed trees.

The river, unwinding across the prairie, was inviting, but Glynette turned her gaze toward the Antelope Mountains to the west. Tom had often described them as a place of enchantment, with bubbling creeks and whispering aspen trees. "Let's go to the mountains."

Tom looked doubtful. "They're nearly ten miles away and off the reserve."

Her eyes sparkled. This information, rather than discouraging her, seemed to make her prefer the destination even more.

"I think Captain McCrae had in mind a short ride along the river."

"But you go to the mountains quite often, don't you? There's no danger."

"You can never be sure."

"Please?"

Tom glanced back toward the fort, looked into her soft, pleading eyes, and shrugged. He was certain to pay the price for taking Mrs. McCrae off the reserve but, gazing into the depths of her eyes, he felt he would rather pay than disappoint her.

"I have to admit, it's a perfect day for the mountains," he said, and turned his horse west.

As they rode, Glynette's heart thrilled with the excitement of an adventure. Everything was so new and strange—the quick flute-like notes of the meadow lark, the funny, gaudy plumage of quarreling magpies, the amorous croaking of ring-necked pheasant cocks. She had never seen such birds before. The fresh, spicy smell of sage and buffalo grass rose to her nostrils, and she breathed deep, thinking it was the cleanest, sweetest smell on earth.

The complexity of the prairie landscape surprised her. What had seemed flat and monotonous in the snow actually rolled and dipped with cattail-choked sloughs, sharp dikes jutting upward from ancient volcanoes, and occasional outcroppings of craggy sandstone. The grasses were dotted with a dozen varieties of tiny wild flowers. Her heart felt lighter than it had in weeks, and the world seemed full of promise.

Suddenly she wished Maggie was with them, though she knew it was impossible. Maggie would spend what remained of her life inside the confines of Fort Reynolds. The realization made her turn to scan the broad, windswept prairie around her. *How short our time is,* she thought. *We must remember to live well while we can.*

"Tom . . ."

He eased his horse closer to hers.

"Can you keep a secret?"

He smiled, an inexplicable sadness in his eyes. "Yes, ma'am. I think I can keep a secret."

"Maggie Lewis is dying." She felt guilty telling Maggie's secret, but it was a relief to share with someone.

"Captain Lewis' wife?"

"Yes. She's been sick for a long time. Now she's worse, and the surgeon can't do anything for her. No one knows about it. Not even Captain Lewis . . . I don't know why I'm telling you. Only that it's so sad."

Tom stared ahead a long moment, squinting against the sun and considering. The sun glinted off the crossed sabers of his forage cap. "Why is she keeping it from her husband? He ought to know."

"I suppose for now they're able to pretend everything is still all right. But once she tells him . . ."

"The man has a right to know."

"Yes, it seems so. But who's to judge . . . ?"

They rode for a while in silence. A flock of geese passed over in a lopsided V—one side longer than the other—their honking resonating in the still prairie air. Glynette dropped behind, watching, then gave her horse a slight dig, bringing it up alongside Tom's.

"I shouldn't have told you. Maggie trusted me," she said.

He smiled the same inexplicable smile. "Your secret is safe. I've never spoken a word to Captain or Mrs. Lewis in my life, and nobody I know would be the least bit interested. We plebe soldiers don't spend much time around officers or their wives—'cept to get orders."

Glynette nodded. It was true. Though she and Tom both called Fort Reynolds home, they inhabited completely different worlds. The officers from West Point and their wives from wealthy Eastern families didn't associate with the enlisted men. For good reason. While the best of the soldiers were poor but honest men who worked a thankless job and risked their lives for little pay, the all-too-common worst of them were a low breed—men who drank themselves into stupors, fought, and mistreated women. Many of them were deserters who reenlisted under assumed names, men who used the Army to hide because they were wanted for theft, assault, and even murder.

She studied Tom's profile and considered what an exception he was to the rule. She was quite certain he was not a drunk or a criminal, and while many soldiers couldn't fulfill their five-year commitment to the frontier Army without going over the hill, he had already finished five years and signed on for another five.

"You spend time with me. I'm an officer's wife."

"Our visits are not of a social nature."

"I consider you my friend." She looked at him seriously, then blushed.

"Well, I thank you for that honor," he said. When she didn't say anything, he glanced at her and realized she thought he was being sarcastic.

"I meant that," he said gently. "It is an honor to be your friend."

Her stomach tightened in the pleasantly uncomfortable way it often did around him, and she looked away. A coyote loped ahead of them, and they watched until it disappeared in the distance, toward the mountains that had begun to draw them in through gently sloping buttes and tree-filled hollows.

"You know, I really don't know anything about you," she said. "Do you have family back in Tennessee?"

He stared straight ahead, expressionless. "They're all dead. 'Cept a niece I never met."

"I'm sorry." It had not occurred to her that Tom was alone in the world, but it explained much that she'd wondered about—the grim, lonely look that rarely left his eyes, his calm acceptance of death and hardship. She didn't dare ask him more, so they rode in silence.

At length Tom spoke again. "Both of my brothers were killed at Shiloh. One outright, the other got his leg amputated and died of infection a month later. My father was so mad, he went off to join the volunteers. I was the youngest, so I stayed on the farm to take care of my mother and sister. When my father was killed at Stone's River that winter, my mother took to her bed and never got up again. I guess she died of grief. So it was just me and my little sister, and when she was fourteen, she married a neighbor boy, so I sold the farm and headed west."

It had all come out in a tumble. He turned to look at her

and gave a short, sad laugh. "I seem to always make you cry."

"Some men will do that, they say," she said, dabbing at her eyes with her handkerchief.

He chuckled. "Funny, that's what I've heard about some women."

Glynette's horse crow-hopped to the left, and she looked down to see a rattlesnake coiled and rattling a warning. She eased her mount away. "So . . . your sister—"

"Died in childbirth. I've never been back to see the child. Her husband remarried, and the little girl is well cared for, I've heard. Seems best to leave it be."

"I think I'd want to see my only family."

"The Army's my family. Has been for seven years. It's a pretty poor substitute, but at least I've got a bed and food and somebody telling me what to do when, so I don't have to think too much."

He stared off into the distance. "Before I joined the Army, I went looking for gold, worked a claim in the mountains by myself. I came down with the fever and lay in my hut for . . . I don't know how long. Weeks. When I came out of it, barely alive, I realized I didn't want to live that kind of life, all alone." He smiled. "I guess that's what makes me appreciate the Army life better than some."

As they approached the mountains, the brush thickened. Small poplars and aspens began to appear along the sides of rivulets trickling alongside the hillsides. They cut up a pass between two steep buttes. Glynette was startled to look up the rise and see bodies tied on platforms in the trees.

"Indians . . . gone to the Land of the Ghosts," Tom informed her.

Three bodies, wrapped in blankets and lashed with

ropes, had been attached to platforms erected high in the trees. The platform and the limbs of the tree around it had been tied with brightly colored bunting, the colors had faded and run together from the rains and melting snow. These were the ghost flags, Tom explained, to keep evil spirits away from the dead. Glynette shivered and fell silent, wondering if she would ever grow used to this strange world called Montana.

At the top of a long rise, a ranch spread out below Glynette and Tom, dreaming in the warm morning sun. A small log cabin nestled in the shade of the cottonwoods and willows of Elk Creek; a large barn, corrals, and several tidy outbuildings spread in the open area nearby. As Tom reined up, he felt the old thrill. He turned to Glynette. "That's Demmer's Ranch. We'll have our lunch there. You can see the new foals."

The morning sun shone warm on the backs of the thirty or so horses grazing on the broad, flat expanse below them. The drowsing horses stood in pairs head to tail, switching flies off themselves and each other. The only sound was the buzzing of the flies, a horse occasionally clearing its nostrils, and the faint far-off scream of a hawk.

Tom and Glynette exchanged glances. He could see the place had the same effect on her as it did him. He loved this ranch nestled against the eastern edge of the Antelope Mountains, with its aspen-lined valleys and meandering creeks. He considered the first day he saw it the luckiest of his life.

As Tom turned his mount toward the corrals in the hollow below them, Glynette followed. Passing between two lines of buffalo skulls lining the trail to the front gate, Glynette saw a young boy, twelve or so, leading a horse around an empty corral by a long rope dallied around a saddle horn. The young bay's sleek dark coat shone like waxed mahogany, and its long tail appeared to have been curry-combed and brushed until there wasn't a snarl in it. Tom whistled appreciatively and said to the boy, "She's a beauty, Will. She'll be ready for a rider soon."

They rode on past the corral to the shade of the barn where Orsen Demmer, a leather-skinned, silver-haired man of about sixty, grinned broadly as they rode up. "Tom Flint! I wasn't expectin' to see you over this way for a while, now you're doin' striker work."

"Howdy, Dem. Meet my boss, Mrs. Captain Anniston McCrae."

The man gave Tom's horse a friendly rub on the neck and turned his grin toward Glynette. He was a wiry, old man but clearly it was lean, hard muscle, and his body moved with a graceful ease. "Glad to meet you, Mrs. McCrae. I don't get too many officer's wives out to the ranch. I feel right honored."

"I've never visited a western ranch, Mr. Demmer, so the honor's mine."

"I'm glad you're here, Tom. That appaloosa is still givin' me fits. He don't have no respect, and here I've been real patient and nice with him and haven't lost my temper or nothin'. Just this mornin' I was wishin' you could give him a ride. My old bones just don't take bein' thrown around like they used to."

"Been bruisin' you up a bit, eh, Dem?"

"A bit," Orsen groused.

"Maybe you ought to go a little slower with 'im. Give 'im some more time to get used to the saddle."

"I ain't got the patience I used to, Tom. That bronc's a hothead, and I ain't gonna coddle a rat-tailed, flea-bitten, hateful cuss like that." He shook his head in disgust. "I'm gettin' too old for this line of work. I ought to be sitting under one of those palm trees in Californy with my sister.

Now, thanks to you, I got three more years of bustin' my—" he glanced at Glynette "—my hide . . . before I get there."

Glynette looked at him quizzically.

"Didn't Tom tell you? He's gonna buy my ranch. I coulda had other buyers, plenty of 'em, but I want Tom to have it."

He cast a scowl at Tom. "Only the . . . the . . ."—he cast a guilty look at Glynette, snorted, and jerked his head toward Tom—". . . the . . . dad-blamed . . . so 'n so . . . went and signed on for another five years with the . . . dad-blamed . . . army."

He released his breath with a puff, his face red from the exertion of spitting out all that frustration without the benefit of a single four-letter word. Glynette looked at Tom, her lips pressed together and eyes bright with repressed laughter.

Tucking his chin under, Tom rolled his eyes up sheepishly, then cut a irritated look at Demmer. "I don't think Mrs. McCrae wants to hear about all that, Dem."

"On the contrary," she said, smiling at Tom. "I'm quite interested, Mr. Demmer. Do go on."

Dem glanced at Tom and hesitated but, encouraged by such an attractive, attentive audience, continued. "Two years ago, Tom coulda mustered out o' the Army and bought this ranch. He had five hundred and forty dollars he'd saved that he coulda put down. Then, hell . . . pardon me, ma'am . . . but, well, heck . . . he coulda taken the next twenty years for all I cared to pay the rest. I knowed he was good for it. But, no, he says it ain't enough, and he goes and signs on for another five years!"

He emphasized the last with a mocking tone and several exaggerated wags of his head. Then he spread his hands and widened his eyes at her appealingly. "In the meantime, I'm gettin' old, Mrs. McCrae. I could be spendin' my winters down in California with my sister instead of freezin' my . . . my bones . . . up here."

Glynette and Dem both looked at Tom, Dem casting a furtive sideways glance, Glynette with eyebrows raised inquisitively, as if waiting for him to defend himself.

Tom sighed and said to Glynette, "Well, what if the ranch didn't make a profit? What if it went bust? There Dem would be in California with no more money comin' in, and I'd be feelin' pretty bad for lettin' down a friend."

He dropped his eyes guiltily, knowing full well that money wasn't the real reason for his signing on to the army for another five. The truth was, when his time came to muster out, he'd been afraid. When the time came, he couldn't stand the thought of going out on his own again.

The signed papers had scarcely left his hand before he knew he'd made a mistake. In a moment of chicken-heartedness, he'd postponed his dream of owning Demmer's ranch for five more years. But he would never admit to Dem that he'd made that colossal mistake because of fear. So he let Dem believe it was because of the money.

"I told ya, Tom, there ain't no way a guy like you ain't gonna make this ranch go." Dem threw up his hands in disgust and looked back at Glynette. "Like talkin' to a brick wall. Don't matter now, anyway. I got three more years to wait, and that's that. Come on, Mrs. McCrae, let's see if we can find you somethin' cold to drink."

He held his arm out for Glynette with an air of self-righteousness. She took his arm with an equally indignant look in Tom's direction, and they marched toward the cabin, Glynette turning her head to smirk at Tom, enjoying herself thoroughly.

Tom wagged his head resignedly, picked up a pail, and headed for the creek.

* * *

Glynette's Corporal

After Tom had watered the horses and Glynette had cooled herself with a glass of tea from a quart jar Dem kept in the spring house behind the cabin, the three of them spread a blanket beneath a cottonwood on the creek bank.

"Well, Tom," Dem said, stretching along one edge of the blanket, "I just got word that Arjay ain't comin' up this year. He's got 'im a girl down in Texas, and he ain't interested in comin' up an' helpin' me no more." He pooched out his lips and looked peevish. "Reckon I'll have to look for a new man."

"Well, you got Arne and Will and me," Tom said. "Why don't you just cut back a bit, Dem? Take it easy."

Dem nodded. "Maybe you're right. Young bucks like Arjay make me tired, anyway. Arne and Will ain't old enough yet to be smart alecks."

Tom chuckled. "Give 'em a couple years." From his knapsack, he pulled shredded beef sandwiches, potato salad, and a jar of bread and butter pickles.

"Army beef again, eh, Tom?" Dem said. "If I'd a known you was comin', I'd a fried us up a nice hen. I know how you get tired of beef. Course if you'd a mustered out when you was supposed to . . ." He let the sentence trail off with a significant look at Glynette.

As he pulled enamel plates and flatware from the bag, Tom cast a guilty look at Glynette. "As soon as the quartermaster will part with the materials, I'm gonna put up a chicken coop in back of Captain and Mrs. McCrae's quarters, so there'll be fresh eggs and chickens all the time."

"Here, let me do that," Glynette said, taking the plates and the knapsack from Tom. "I certainly don't mind beef, but what I do miss are fresh vegetables."

"The garden's tilled and seeded," Tom said, watching as Glynette set a plate, fork, and napkin before each of them, then rustle through the knapsack for a spoon for the potato salad. "Won't be long before you're eatin' fresh greens and sweet peas."

She looked up, spoon in hand, and smiled into Tom's eyes. "Now that sounds heavenly. I've already had my fill of canned beans and canned peaches."

"Sounds like Tom's doin' a right good job for you, eh, Mrs. McCrae?" said Dem, holding up his plate while Glynette dipped potato salad onto it.

"He's a marvel, Mr. Demmer."

Dem smiled his approval. "Well, now, I reckon you got a discerning eye, ma'am. You'll find that Tom's a man of many talents. I knew right away the first time I met him that he was exceptional."

Sensing what was coming, Tom said, "Dem, I don't think Mrs. McCrae wants to hear—"

But it was too late. Dem had already started in with his story, and neither Glynette nor Dem was paying Tom any attention.

"Shortly after Tom joined the Army," Dem told Glynette, "he and two other greenhorns were assigned to fetch some fresh mounts from me. The lieutenant heading up the detail knew nothin' an' gave me a bigger hoot than a bunch of raw cavalry recruits who could barely stay on a horse, so I figured we were in for some good fun with these three."

Glynette grinned at Tom as Dem went on telling how he had offered to let the recruits have a try at his most ornery bronc. As expected, the other two soldiers had been quickly and unceremoniously tossed. Then Tom mounted. The horse bucked and reared, stalled, twisted and rolled, but Tom stuck to the saddle through the horse's most violent efforts to shake him. The joke had been on Dem because the lieutenant hadn't told him that Tom, who'd been raised on a ranch and spent his child-

Glynette's Corporal

hood around horses, could handle a mount better than most cavalry officers.

Dem shook his head, grinning at the memory. "I told the lieutenant, 'I want that boy,' and he convinced the post commander that it would be in the Army's best interest to detail Tom to some work at the ranch."

Glynette smiled at Tom. "I had no idea."

"Mrs. McCrae, I tell you true," Dem said solemnly, "that horse bowed to Tom in respect when the ride was over."

Glynette raised her brows. "Bowed?"

"Yeah," Tom said wryly, "then gave my boot a kiss."

Dem cackled. "Well, how 'bout we see if you can make that appaloosa kiss your boot?"

After clearing the dishes, Glynette clung to the side of the corral, watching Tom work. Dem had helped Tom wrestle a saddle onto the bronc, then climbed out of the corral. He watched with Glynette as the bronc tried every manner of bucking and scraping Tom off his back. After half an hour Tom was white with dust.

Glynette still wasn't sure who was winning when Tom yelled to Will, "Open the gate, kid. Let's air 'im out."

Will grinned, swung the gate open, pulled his hat from his head and swung it in the air with a whoop. When the bronc saw the gap he charged out at a run. Dem, who had hooked a boot heel on the fence, guffawed and slapped a hand against his dusty thigh. "That's my boy! Ain't he somethin' to see?"

"Yes, he is, Mr. Demmer."

Dem turned to Glynette who shielded her eyes against the sun and watched Tom's quickly diminishing figure, her features creased with concern.

"Don't you worry about 'ol Tom," Dem said gently. "I ain't seen the horse yet that was a match for him."

She smiled. "I'm not worried. I envy him . . . and you too."

Dem chuckled. "Why in the world would you do that?"

"The two of you live according to your nature, unfettered by civilization and its conventions." She glanced at him, wondering if he had any idea what she meant. "I envy you because you have only these beautiful mountains for company, and they do not care if you are proper or not."

Dem furrowed his brow. "That seems like a strange thing for a fine Eastern lady such as yourself to say. You have . . . nice things . . . an easy life."

She laughed. "Would you rather be 'a fine Eastern lady' with my 'easy life' than a man like yourself living a life such as yours?"

"Well, no, not when you put it like that." He scratched his head.

Glynette continued to stare toward where Tom had disappeared. She breathed in a deep breath of the dusty, sage-smelling air. "Me either, Mr. Demmer."

Glynette was reluctant to leave the ranch and the happiness she'd found there, even when Tom pointed out that it was getting late. She was persuaded to leave only after coercing a promise from Tom that they would come again the following day. On the ride home, her heart felt near to exploding with joy. Every sight, smell, and sound seemed to vibrate through her senses into her soul. She had not felt so delighted with life, so full of emotion, for years.

A strange and poignant melancholy lay beneath the joy, but even it felt strangely sweet. The clear light slanting across the rocks and sagebrush cast long, moody shadows that filled her with an inexplicable longing. Now and then Tom turned to her, as though to make sure she was all right. His sad, gentle smile warmed her. He seemed to share her mood, a mood in harmony with the landscape, the universe. She did not want the feeling to end.

It was nearly dusk when Tom and Glynette drew up their mounts before the McCraes' quarters. Glynette slipped from the black, handing her reins to Tom, and entered the dark house. The room was lit only by a flickering fire. She saw Anniston's long shadow projected over the wall and ceiling, the grotesque outline growing and shrinking as he paced. At the sight of him, she felt the last ember of her joy snuffed.

He turned as she approached. "How was your ride?"

She couldn't tell if he was angry. "It was lovely." She tensed, hoping he would not inquire about their destination.

He looked her up and down, studied her face. "I'm glad, as that will be your last ride for a while."

She grasped the back of a chair, her knees suddenly weak. He wanted to punish her for being late, she thought. "What do you mean?"

"Our battalion is to be put in readiness for immediate field service. We're leaving tomorrow."

She blinked, trying to grasp his meaning. Something had happened. Some disaster had occurred. "I thought there was to be no summer campaign."

He lifted his chin. "This morning a man rode in . . . full of arrows. The Tin Creek Station was attacked, and he was the only one to make it out alive. I don't think you want to know the details. Suffice it to say that the station has been burned and three men have been brutally killed at the hands of savages."

Glynette's mind was numb. She had known this would happen at some point. It was what Anniston had come west for, to glorify himself in the fight against the Indians, secure his future in Washington, and perhaps— she knew he thought it—immortalize himself in the annals of history.

"We're taking all of the Second's troops," Anniston continued, "but two men from each will stay to tend stable duties. I'll leave Tom, so you won't be alone. Companies G and H Infantry will garrison."

"The wilderness is so vast. How will you ever find them?"

Anniston nodded sagely. "They'll be easy to track. They stole mules, guns, and supplies." He smiled, grasping her shoulders, but his eyes were more cold and ruthless than she had ever seen them. They were the eyes of a man wanting to kill. "Either they'll surrender, or they'll fight us, and we will obliterate them."

He drew close to her, staring, his nose wrinkling in distaste. "You've gone and burned your skin, Glynette. You look dreadful. It's just as well you won't be riding any more." He released her.

Glynette instinctively drew her hand to her cheek. The skin felt tight. Even with the protection of a wide-brimmed hat, her skin was unaccustomed to a long day in the prairie sun. "I'll put cream on," she stammered, self-conscious under her husband's disapproving gaze.

Anniston silently turned toward the fire, seeming to forget her.

A faint rattle of pans came from the kitchen annex. Seeing that Anniston had drifted off into a private reverie, she walked down the short hallway to the kitchen. Tom was standing in front of the stove, tending a skillet of sizzling bacon.

The now-familiar sight of his auburn hair curling against his sunburned neck comforted her. "Can I do anything to help?"

He tilted his head toward the small wooden table behind him. "You could chop those potatoes if you want."

She picked up a knife and sliced a potato in two. "Did you hear?" she asked.

He nodded and set a loaf of bread on the table beside the potatoes. "I heard."

"Do you wish you were going?"

He looked up, knife poised above the loaf of bread, and chuffed. "Why in the world would I wish that?"

"Dem says you've fought bravely against the Indians in the past. I thought perhaps you liked it."

He looked thoughtfully at her, then carved a thick slice of bread from the loaf. "No, I didn't like it. I just didn't want to die. I didn't want anybody else to die."

"You aren't sorry that you'll be left behind?"

He stared at her for so long that she swallowed and wondered what Anniston would think if he walked into the kitchen. The knife remained in mid-air above the forgotten loaf of bread.

"No," he said at last, "I'm not."

Chapter Four

Well before gunfire and the reveille bugle, Anniston was up, shaving and scenting himself with his habitual care and elegance. Glynette lay awake watching him, feeling the strain that already seemed to emanate from the entire garrison, as they all anxiously awaited roll call and inspection, and dreaded the moment when the battalion would march off to the sound of drum and fife.

When Anniston had completed his toilet, he stood back from the mirror and brushed a speck of dust from his coat sleeve. He smoothed his long, blond mustache, guiding it into place with his thumb.

Glynette sat on the edge of the bed and stretched, then dropped her feet into her slippers. "I'll tell Tom to put breakfast on the table." She slid into her wrapper and tied it.

"Dress first," Anniston said curtly, pulling on his field boots.

"Anniston—" she began in protest.

"Mrs. McCrae," he said with exaggerated patience, "I am leaving today and will be gone indefinitely. In my absence, I expect you to obey the rules I have given you." His smile was patronizing. "Is that too much to ask?"

Glynette's Corporal

Her lips parted, but she said nothing. She started to turn away, but he caught her by the elbow and spun her toward him. "Is that too much to ask?"

She stared at him with wide, wondering eyes. In recent weeks she had come to accept that she could never win Anniston's affection and had begun to resign herself to a sham marriage. Divorce was essentially unthinkable. It would scandalize her family and destroy her mother. But if her husband could not love her, she wished that he would at least leave her in peace.

"What rules do you mean, Anniston?" she asked. "You mean not sitting at the breakfast table in my wrapper?"

"Yes, Glynette," he said, spacing his words and forcing them through compressed lips, as though she were too thick to follow his meaning. "You will dress for breakfast. You will fulfill your social obligations. You will not leave the fort. You will remember that you are in command of nothing except the servant." He turned toward the mirror and dusted imaginary flakes from his shoulders.

She sighed. "Certainly I will follow your rules, Anniston, but I ask that you not confine me to the fort."

"As my wife you will adhere to all my rules without question."

"Not that one."

He reached her in two quick strides and caught up the cord and tassel of her silk wrapper. "Don't argue with me, Glynette. Three men were brutally murdered not twenty miles from here. How in Hades can you even think of going out there?"

She stumbled, then yanked at the cord in his hand, and tried to push him away. His gaze, black with menace, frightened her. "I can think of going out there," she said, "because I know there is no real danger this close to the fort, and I will die if I have to stay in here."

"You will die if you do not do as I say," he said, letting

the words linger and watching her eyes widen as she wondered at his meaning. Then he added, "At least, if you get yourself captured by Indians you will wish you were dead."

He released the cord and turned away. She shuddered. By now she knew that Anniston did not love her, but she had not realized how much he hated her. The hate in his eyes was terrifying. "You care nothing for my safety, Anniston," she whispered. "Why do you pretend to?"

Suddenly he turned and lunged at her. He clenched her arm in his left hand, and raised his right. She winced at the pain in her left wrist. It felt as if it might break. The pain was too great for her to even try to wrench the arm away.

"Anniston," she gasped, "my arm . . ."

His grip tightened, and her vision went black. Her knees went weak.

"Am I getting through to you, Glynette?"

She hesitated. "Yes," she gasped.

He made a barking sound that was meant to be a laugh. "You little liar." He raised his hand again.

Tears burned her eyes, but she lifted her chin. "Do you mean to . . . hit me, Anniston?"

"I will do whatever I must to get through to you," he said through gritted teeth.

She flinched, frightened by the fury in his gaze, but spoke with careful deliberation. "If you hit me, Anniston, I will divorce you. If you do not release my arm now, I will divorce you."

He couldn't care less about losing her, she knew, but divorce would sully his reputation and ruin his career. It would be the last thing he'd want. She braced herself for his reaction.

He sucked in his breath and rolled his eyes. His face turned red, and he swung to the side, releasing the grip on her arm. "You cursed, worthless woman," he cried, each syllable coming like the crack of a whip—sharp, snapping. "Why did you vow to obey me only to war with me from the beginning?"

Ignoring his outburst, she cradled her injured arm and continued with a softness that belied the force of her words. "I no longer expect love from you, Anniston, or even respect. I've given up hope for a real marriage between us. But in place of that, I will make my own rules. Do not try to confine me to this fort because I will slip out anyway, and everyone will know that I have defied you."

She continued to stare at him, her gaze unwavering, but not defiant. She didn't want a battle, just a peaceful coexistence with this hard man with whom she must live out her life.

He stared at her with a look of hatred that shriveled her heart. "You are not fit to have as a wife."

"I do not feel that I have gained a prize in you either."

He expelled a bitter laugh and turned on her, his lip curled in a sneer. "I have given you my success and my fortune." He pointed a finger at her. "You have given me nothing. You . . ." He turned away, looking for the right words. "You are inept as an officer's wife. You have no polish, no wit, no style. You are a drag on my career."

Glynette lowered her eyes. So it had come to this. They would say all the bitter things they had only hinted at before, and their marriage would be one of open hate. She hesitated, then willed herself to turn to the stairs without a word. She had reached the door when she remembered she was still in her wrapper and had been forbidden to go downstairs. Her mouth twisted in a wry smile. She turned back to face him.

"You have given me nothing, Anniston," she said. "I care nothing for your name or your ambitions. I never have. I cared only for my father . . . it was his wish that I should marry you."

Her heart felt heavy at the thought of her father. His heart would be broken if he could see them now. The memory of him had always kept her trying to salvage her relationship with Anniston. Lately, however, she found herself thinking that, though well intentioned, her father had been a bit of a fool. She had spent the whole of her marriage altering herself to please Anniston. Only Anniston was never pleased, and she was tired of trying.

"Though you have tried to stamp out my interests, my friends, my desires," she continued, "I have born your demands with equanimity, Anniston, and tried to be a good wife."

"A good wife!" He laughed derisively. "You are a consummate failure as a wife, Glynette, wholly unfit to represent a man in my position, yet you make no effort to improve yourself. You do not even care that you have failed to give me a child."

She stared at him coldly. He had said many cruel things to her in the two years of their marriage, but he had not yet blamed their childlessness on her. She started to suggest that if he acted more as a husband to her, a child might come. Instead she found herself saying, "Perhaps you would find me more appealing, Anniston, if I wore feathers and painted my face."

She looked at him full on as she spoke to see the effect of her words. She'd put it together weeks ago—Lucy's insinuating hints about Anniston's visits to the Indian camp, his strange disappearances during the day, his lack of desire for her. He had hardly touched her since she had come to the fort.

By the look on her husband's face she knew that what the women whispered was true—he was unfaithful. She shouldn't have been surprised. Half the men she knew were rumored to visit prostitutes. They knew their wives had no choice but to accept it. Divorce would mean sacrificing their own and their children's security and dignity. Anniston figured he could do as he pleased.

Anniston flushed. "I don't know what nonsense you're talking, Glynette." But her lance had hit its mark, she could tell, and for the moment she had the upper hand. It gave her no joy, for she realized this moment marked the final blow to their marriage. She no longer cared to pretend that she and Anniston had anything resembling a marriage. She had sensed it coming, had feared it, but now that it had arrived, she felt an unexpected surge of strength. How dare he presume to lay down rules for her?

"I do command more than the servant, Anniston," she said, her voice tremulous with unfamiliar emotions. "From this moment forward, I command my own fate."

He stared at her, his eyes enlarging 'til it seemed they would pop from his skull. Then, in a single movement, he leaned forward and swept the bottles, brushes, and ornaments from her dressing table. They slammed against the wall, shattering, and scattered over the floor.

"You are not fit to live," he thundered, his footsteps on the stairs like pistol shots. "And I will command your fate."

The sky was like a pink pearl. Even at dawn the air was warm, and the May day promised to be unusually hot. Glynette stood on the veranda, eyes shaded against the early morning sun, and pushed her muslin sleeve up her long, delicate arm. Seeing the dark, painful bruise running in splotches up her forearm, she quickly pulled the sleeve back down.

She watched the crowds gather. Down the row of verandas beside her, the officers' wives emerged from their houses in their finest dresses, their children fresh in

Sunday clothes, damp hair neatly combed. On the porches of the barracks, the soldiers who were to remain in garrison milled, hooting and yelling lewd expletives at their departing brethren. Around the outside of the barracks porches, laundresses and Indian women, with broods of dirty children, waited anxiously for their lovers and husbands to march off to battle.

Glynette felt a tug at her elbow and looked up to see the broad grin of Gregor Britzman. He propped a beefy thigh on the railing that separated his side of the veranda from hers and smiled at her warmly. Like Anniston, he was in field dress—flannel shirt, black, wide-brimmed felt hat, and blue trousers tucked in at the knees into trooper boots.

"Well, here we are, Glynette. Your first summer expedition. What do you think?"

She cast her eyes toward the parade ground, hard-packed from frequent drilling, where the soldiers were falling in with their respective companies to form lines, the younger recruits looking a little bewildered as they struggled with their mounts.

"I think—"

Before she could say what she thought, Anniston and Infantry Captain Frank Allen Sherry stepped onto the veranda beside Gregor. Anniston dropped a heavy hand on Gregor's shoulder and sneered in Glynette's direction, but she didn't look at him. The sneer shriveled into a look of icy hatred. He turned to Gregor. "It's almost show time, old chap. Are we ready?"

Gregor chuckled and lifted his chin toward the parade. "Just look at 'em. It's been a long winter. These boys are ready for the field."

Anniston chuckled appreciatively and pulled Captain Sherry toward Glynette. When the captain doffed his hat and smiled, she gave him her hand. He held it too long,

Glynette's Corporal

and would not release it when she attempted discreetly to tug it away. A heavy diamond ring flashed on his little finger. She did not care for Captain Sherry. He often belittled his wife under the guise of humor. She had heard him cut off Dinah's contributions to dinner conversation with a haughty laugh, exclaiming, "Come now, you distracted little goose! Who has filled your head with such nonsense?"

To his credit, his wife was indeed a fool, a menacing one at that, the post's worst gossip, needing only the word of an indiscreet servant to start the most malicious rumors. But that did not excuse Captain Sherry. He seemed to transfer his low opinion of his wife to all women, and he had a bold, insinuating expression that Glynette found unnerving.

"Captain Sherry's company will be among the unfortunates holding down the fort," Anniston said. He grinned at Sherry, then turned to Glynette. "If you need anything, dear, let Frank know," he said, his tone solicitous, his eyes frosty.

Captain Sherry, handsome with his oiled black hair and heavy black mustache trimmed dragoon style, nodded and gave her hand a slow squeeze. "I'm at your beck and call, Mrs. McCrae. I have orders from Major Dixon to make sure the ladies are happy and well attended in his absence."

"That's quite a job, Captain." Glynette smiled politely and jerked her hand free. "I wish you luck."

Anniston rested a hand on Captain Sherry's shoulder and turned to Glynette with an unnatural smile. "You should know that if the fort comes under attack, Sherry and the other officers remaining have orders to kill you immediately."

Gregor jerked his head up, eyes bulging, and made a slight choking sound.

He glanced quickly at Glynette, then Anniston. Good

God, he thought, what a thing to bring up now! Certainly Glynette knew the wives were to be shot rather than captured by Indians—a quick death being more agreeable than torture at the hands of the savages. In fact, the more experienced Army wives carried derringers for the purpose of taking their own and their children's lives if abducted. But to bring it up at a time like this in such a cavalier fashion. Then Gregor saw the cold light in Anniston's eyes and realized that he was trying to humiliate Glynette to make some point.

"Anniston," Gregor began, "Perhaps this isn't the time—"

"What better time?" Anniston interjected, turning on the subaltern with a cold look. Gregor returned the stare for a moment before glancing sympathetically at Glynette and turning his attention to the parade.

Glynette waited. Gregor kept his eyes glued to the parade. Captain Sherry turned attentively to Anniston who continued, "You see, my dear. A captured woman who is not instantly killed by the savages in the most gruesome way will invariably be beaten and passed into servitude."

Anniston raised his eyebrows at Sherry as if expecting corroboration. Sherry cut his eyes between the two men, cleared his throat, and turned to Glynette. "Uh, yes, when white women are returned from the hands of Indians, what is returned alive is, in the main, wreckage. No woman who has experienced abduction and captivity returns as the same person. The damage cannot be repaired." He smiled.

"That's precisely what I was explaining to Glynette this morning when I told her she must stay inside the fort until the renegades are subdued," Anniston said. He added in a deadly low voice, "I do not believe I convinced her, however."

Glynette stared at him in silence. She did not know what he meant to accomplish with this display. She didn't care. In a few minutes he would be gone.

Gregor cleared his throat and, casting a glance toward the parade, said, "The bugler's about to blow, Captain. It's time."

Anniston continued to hold Glynette's gaze, then lifted his chin and said, "Right-o." Turning stiffly, he stepped from the veranda as the bugle sounded. Sherry doffed his hat again in Glynette's direction and descended the steps behind Anniston.

When they were gone, Gregor leaned over and put a hand gently on Glynette's shoulder. He smiled sadly. Glynette stiffened and gritted her teeth, trying to keep the tears from spilling over. "I'll miss you, Gregor."

His throat tightened. He wanted to say so much to her, something to erase the sorrow he knew she silently endured as the wife of Anniston McCrae. "Hold down the fort, Glynette. We'll be home soon." He kissed her cheek, then turned to follow Anniston onto the parade.

Anniston mounted and rode before lines of young men sporting freshly scrubbed faces and clean blue uniforms trimmed in gold piping. The soldiers sat atop rows of chestnuts, grays, and blacks whose coats had been groomed until their glossy skins shone in the sun like cut velvet and their manes lay smooth. Sabers and rifles, buttons and boots, had all been cleaned and polished. Captain McCrae paced his horse up and down in front of the line, his back slightly arched, admiring his troops. His self-conscious pose suggested that, over and above his military interests, his appearance occupied a considerable space in his thoughts.

"That husband of yours is every inch a soldier and every inch a man."

Glynette heard the grating voice of Lucy Britzman behind her and realized that she'd been so distracted by Anniston's parting words that she hadn't heard the screen door of the Britzmans' quarters open and slam shut. She turned now to see Lucy, stuffed into dotted muslin ruffled with Valenciennes, her fat feet stuffed into a pair of bronze kid boots. She twirled a matching dotted, ruffled parasol and stared out over the parade in Anniston's direction.

"Good morning, Lucy," Glynette said, trying to sound cordial. How was it that someone she adored as much as she adored Gregor could be married to someone she detested as much as she detested Lucy? "I didn't hear you come out."

Lucy smiled at her with benevolent understanding. "Dinah says you aren't coming to the luncheon today."

"That's right. I'm going riding."

"Oh, look, there's Dinah now." Lucy looked down the row of officers' houses and waved.

Two houses up Dinah Sherry and Sibyl Nye stood on Sibyl's veranda. "Come, let's join them," Lucy said. She turned and put her head in the door. "Dolly!" she shrieked. The Pomeranian's toenails sounded on the stairs. "Come along, Dolly. Let's go visiting."

Glynette did not care one way or the other about joining the other ladies. The only reason she had ever cared to have them like her was to please Anniston, and now she didn't care if Anniston was pleased. That, at least, was a pleasant feeling. But, since she didn't mind, she stepped down and fell in beside Lucy and Dolly.

As they approached the Nyes' quarters, Dinah exclaimed, "I hear you're not coming to my luncheon today, Mrs. McCrae." She stuck out her lip in an exaggerated pout.

"I'm sorry, Dinah," Glynette said, as she mounted the porch stairs, "but I had already made plans to go riding."

"Well, I know you must try to distract yourself from your sorrow and loneliness at such a time." Dinah's voice dripped with sarcasm. "Is your striker—I can't remember his name—escorting you? I saw you leaving with him yesterday."

No doubt you did, Glynette thought. In the short time she had been at Fort Reynolds, she had learned that no one had any secrets. The walls were thin, the confines of the fort were small, everyone was bored, and gossip was rampant.

"His name is Tom, and yes, he will escort me."

Dinah smiled insinuatingly. "Of course."

Glynette returned her attention to the parade ground, determined not to let Dinah's insinuations ruin her day. On the parade, Anniston had stopped before Company B. He scowled and stared a moment, then approached the mounted company sergeant. "Sergeant Kyle!" he shouted, his voice exploding like a rifle shot.

The sergeant tightened the reins on his startled mount and saluted. Except that he flushed deeply and his eyes started from their sockets, Kyle faced the captain's furious scowl with soldierly stoicism.

"Sergeant Kyle, your troops are not in uniform!" Anniston McCrae shouted for everyone to hear.

Kyle's eyes involuntarily strayed to the men in line behind him, then snapped back to Captain McCrae. "Sir, I don't understand, sir," he said loudly enough to avoid reprimand, but not loud enough for everyone on the parade to hear.

"Those boots!" Anniston boomed. He jerked his head toward one of the nearest soldiers. "At least six of your men are wearing non-regulation boots."

Kyle cleared his throat and stuck out his chin. "Sir, the men needed new boots for the expedition. The quartermaster ran out. These were the only ones we could get, sir."

After a pause, McCrae shouted to everyone around him, "Then let's hang the quartermaster!"

Lucy cackled. "That Anniston! Hang the quartermaster! My word!"

Everyone laughed heartily, since it was clearly what Captain McCrae wanted. Everyone except Major Johnson, who stood mounted to the far side overseeing the inspection. He did not find such displays amusing, for they led to a general air of disrespect. But if Captain McCrae noticed that the major's face remained stony, he didn't show it. Obviously delighted with his own irascibility, he walked his mount through the battalion seeking some further pretext for his wrath. After upbraiding one noncom for his unpolished saber, another for the unevenness of his column, he seemed pleased enough with himself and the general order of things.

Glynette sat down in a wicker rocker. Lucy looked at her suspiciously. "Don't you feel like watching, dear?"

"I just feel like sitting a moment." She could no longer watch Anniston's callous, narcissistic display.

Maggie, carrying Ned, stepped onto the porch. She smiled and greeted the ladies in turn. Glynette could see that she looked pale and knew she was taking Jim's departure hard.

"I'm awfully late," Maggie gasped as she plopped into the chair next to Glynette, "but Ned was being so cranky this morning that the girls couldn't get him dressed or fed." She stuffed Ned into Glynette's outstretched arms. "I'm pooped."

"Shush, the band's starting," Lucy said. As the band played a rousing medley of Army songs, the sun climbed over the barracks, tinging everything red and setting fire to the brass of the band. Lucy pulled a lump of molasses candy from her pocket.

"Waltz for the ladies, Dolly," Lucy commanded, show-

Glynette's Corporal

ing the Pomeranian the candy. The women had all seen the trick before, but they laughed appreciatively as the little dog stood on his hind legs and performed a series of unsteady circles.

Glynette bounced Ned to the music and pointed to the pretty horses, but her emotions were strangely flat. It did not seem real to her that the troops were going off to fight renegade Indians. And though her mind knew that something irrevocable had happened between her and Anniston, she felt nothing.

She watched impassively as the troops prepared to depart. At last the cannon fired, Major Johnson shouted the order, and the troops—cavalry first, brought up by the artillery and infantry—began their parade around the grounds to the strains of "The Girl I Left Behind Me." Finally they marched through the gates and across the plains, to the hinterland somewhere to the northwest, where the renegades were rumored to be.

After the columns of troops had disappeared beyond the horizon, Tom leaned against a post on the porch of the cavalry barracks feeling, like most everyone else left behind, an unshakeable malaise. He took comfort in the fort's familiar odors of stables, sagebrush, dust, gun oil, and sweat-soaked wool, but the barracks were silent and deserted. A carriage pushed by a nursemaid trundled along officers' row. There was not a man in sight. All of Troop E were gone, all the friends with whom he could break the silence and dispel the mood.

At 7:30 the bugler stepped from the adjutant's office to call the remaining men to first fatigue. They emerged from here and there, scurrying off to their assigned details of repairing roofs, tending livestock, or cleaning washrooms. Tom alone stood on the barracks porch, unhurried. His new position as a striker gave him a freedom he had not known before in the Army. In Captain McCrae's absence, his primary duty was to serve and protect Mrs. McCrae.

Tom was wary of being alone with the captain's wife. The beautiful young woman from Washington had awakened feelings he had never known. Before now, he'd mostly avoided thinking about women. Army pay was poor and married housing scarce, making it almost impossible for an enlisted man to marry, so he'd always considered himself married to the Army.

He'd been in love only once. The fall after he enlisted, he had begun courting a rancher's daughter north of the Missouri River. She was a pretty, tomboyish girl named Lorraine who could ride and rope as well as any man. Though she was lean and muscular from hard work, her flannel shirt and jeans nevertheless shaped themselves into the curves of a woman. He'd had a long, slow courtship with Lorri, visiting her whenever he could, and they'd planned to marry when his Army contract was up.

But he'd had more than three years to go, and that proved to be too long for Lorri. He could ride out to her father's ranch to see her only when he could get a three-day pass. She had been contented enough with that for the first couple of years, but as she became more of a woman, she grew restless, and finally one of her father's cowhands caught Lorri's eye.

Tom sighed and chuckled at the memory. It had been painful at the time, but he had plunged himself into his work and later realized that it had been for the best. Lorraine was a pretty, affectionate woman who knew horses and who wasn't afraid of hard work. She'd have been the perfect rancher's wife, and that was just what he had wanted, for he'd already made up his mind then that Orsen Demmer's ranch would some day be his own. But in hindsight he saw there had been something missing between him and Lorri, that indefinable sympathy that drew people together for life. He guessed that's why it had been easy enough for her to forget him and take up with some cowpoke.

Tom ran a hand through his auburn hair and squinted his eyes toward the horizon, feeling suddenly anxious to ride out to Dem's, to get away from the fort. But he had seen Mrs. McCrae walk Maggie Lewis to her quarters and figured she would be visiting awhile.

It wasn't good the way he longed to see her, he knew, the way he was looking forward to spending the day on horseback by her side. The more time he spent alone with her, the more he would care for her... he shook his head as though to shake away the thought. With a ragged sigh, he pushed himself off the railing and sauntered down the walk in the direction of the McCraes' quarters.

Two hours later Tom and Glynette rode side by side out of Fort Reynolds. They had just reached the foothills when a bank of heavy, purple clouds came creeping over the tops of the Antelope Mountains. The clouds folded in on themselves as they came, swelling massively above the trailing tendrils of white that scudded along at an alarming speed beneath them.

"You were right about the storm," Glynette said, as they felt the first blast of wind from the front. She was not yet used to the enormity of the Montana sky, nor the violent appearance of a storm approaching through that boundless expanse.

"It's all right. We have a few minutes," Tom said reassuringly, but he was irritated with himself for letting her talk him into coming out here when they could see clouds forming in the west. It seemed like lately he'd lost all his common sense. He pointed to his right. "We'll cut over to the main road. There's a roadhouse there we can stop at until the storm blows over."

They turned their mounts in the direction Tom had pointed. "Hurry!" Tom shouted above the wind. He kicked his horse into a gallop.

The roadhouse, barn, and corral sat along a barren stretch of road in a shallow valley between two tawny ridges. High brush and cattails stretched behind the compound, showing a dry watercourse. Several saddled horses stood in the corral, their coats glistening wetly as the rain bounced off their backs.

"Come on!" Tom yelled to Glynette as they galloped into the yard and headed for the corral. "Go to the house," he told her, dismounting and reaching for her reins.

Head down, Glynette ran to the low-slung, weather-beaten roadhouse as Tom loosened the saddle cinches and turned the horses into the corral. He ran to the house, boots splashing in the puddles forming on the hard-packed, hay-flecked yard, and found Glynette waiting for him on the gallery.

"You're soaked," Tom said, pushing open the door. He stepped aside to let Glynette enter before him.

"Ralph, you got a couple towels?" he asked the man who ran the place, even before his eyes got used to the smoky darkness.

"Just a minute, Tom," a big man in a greasy white apron said in a faint German accent. He delivered bowls of stew to the four men sitting at a table against the back wall.

He returned, grinning—a big, swarthy man with thinning gray hair, liver spots on his face, and a missing front tooth. "You got caught in the rain, eh? Them too." He jerked a thumb at the men sitting at the table, as hard-looking a foursome as Tom had ever seen. "Rain not too good for travelers, but good for me, eh? Ha ha ha!"

The man disappeared into the kitchen and returned with

two threadbare towels. "This is all I have. Sorry." He smiled at Glynette as his overtly appraising eyes ran down her trim, high-busted figure. Her clothes clung to her, Tom noticed, and wisps of wet hair stuck in ringlets to her neck.

"This yours?" Ralph asked Tom, indicating Glynette, who stopped toweling her hair to blush and slide her eyes toward Tom.

Tom flushed. "Ralph, this is Mrs. McCrae. I work for her and her husband, Captain McCrae, over at the fort."

Unabashed, the big man laughed and held out his hand. "I see," he said, as Glynette shook his hand. "I'm Ralph Anderson. I run this place. Tom stops by now and then on his way to see ol' Demmer. Sometimes he brings me antelope he shot, and I give him free meals and beer." He turned his small, pale eyes to Tom. "You bring me any meat today?"

Tom was running his towel brusquely over his wet head. "Sorry, Ralph."

"Maybe next time. You and the lady have a seat, and I bring some stew. How 'bout beer? You want beer?"

Tom glanced at Glynette. "No, thank you," she said, her lips tugging into a wry smile.

She turned to look at her surroundings. She'd never seen such a place, and couldn't stop running her eyes across the dim, shabby room furnished mostly with handmade, rough-hewn tables and chairs, and smoking lanterns hanging from bowed ceiling beams. Behind the bar, which was several planks draped over wooden kegs, hung a long rectangular portrait of a woman reclining on a fainting couch clad in only a blue boa.

"I'll have a beer," Tom said. "Why don't you bring Mrs. McCrae a sarsparilla?"

As Tom led Glynette to a table, one of the foursome sitting against the wall said, "That one can sit at my table any day of the week."

Another gave a soft hoot. "She can sit on my knee!"

All four laughed loudly. Glynette looked at Tom, whose eyes told her to ignore them. "I shouldn't have brought you here," he said.

"No," Glynette said with an air of distraction, looking around the room but avoiding the foursome, "this is . . . something new for me."

"Yeah, sorry about that too."

"Really," she said. She turned her eyes to his, wet hair sliding against her face. "I like it."

"Just the same, we'll be on our way as soon as the rain lets up. These gullywashers never last very long."

Glynette reached across the table and placed her hand on his. "Will you please relax. I'm not going to faint or get hysterical. This is good for me."

Tom studied her. She was a new one on him. As elegant a woman as he'd ever seen, yet she regarded her roughneck surroundings with wide-eyed enthusiasm, like a child. He had a brief, melancholy thought that he'd always find every other woman lacking now that he had met her.

"What are you thinking about?" she said.

Suddenly he realized she'd caught him staring. He looked away, flushing. "Nothing."

"Tell me."

He looked at her and took a breath, trying to come up with something fast. "Horses," he said and faked a grin.

Her eyes stayed on his but the smile faded from her lips.

"Here we go—beer for you and sarsparilla for the lady," Ralph said, setting the drinks before them. Tom smiled up at him, half-relieved and half-annoyed by the rescue.

Silently, Tom and Glynette sipped their drinks. Ralph

Glynette's Corporal

brought two bowls of stew and a plate of corn bread, and they ate. As they ate, they avoided each other's eyes.

Finally Tom swiped the last of the gravy with his bread and stuffed it in his mouth. He was still chewing when one of the foursome loudly cleared his throat.

"Yeah, that is a fine looking woman that bluecoat's with," he said, loud enough for his voice to carry to the horses in the corral.

"Where do you suppose a bluebelly come up with such a fine-lookin' girl as that?" another piped up.

"I don't know," still another man said. "Maybe he kidnapped her off her daddy's porch."

Tom's face flushed as he turned his eyes to Glynette, who watched him expectantly. "I think we'd best go," he said, sliding back his chair. Furtively, he reached his right hand down to his holster and snapped the cover loose.

One of the hardcases said, "How 'bout it, miss? Did this big, ol' bluebelly here kidnap you?"

Glynette looked at them coldly.

"Come on," Tom said, taking her arm and leading her toward the door.

"I think she needs us to intervene!" one of the hardcases intoned, grabbing the table and staggering to his feet. The table jerked, clinking empty glasses together. Beer sloshed from a full one.

Tom stopped, pulling Glynette behind him, and stepped over to the man. His eyes were dark and his jaw was set. "Why don't you just sit back down and behave yourself?" he asked the man, whose dirty jeans and tattered hide vest bespoke a drover, probably drifting between jobs, looking for trouble to fill his time. He was wiry, with a thick, curly red beard and a high forehead. His filthy flannel shirt, open to the belly, showed a matt of reddish hair on his sinewy chest. His eyes had the glassy, unfocused quality of a drunk.

The man's eyes widened and darkened with anger. "Don't tell me what to do, soldier boy . . . or I'll clean your clock right here and now."

Tom glanced at the other three. Drifting cowboys, or men on the dodge. They had a cutthroat look about them. He knew he was in trouble, and his mind worked quickly, sizing up each man.

In a reasonable tone, the man on the far side of the table—a stocky, black-haired, black-mustached man with a red bandanna around his neck—said, "Why don't you turn the little lady over to us for safekeepin'?" He smiled.

The man's shoulder moved almost imperceptibly. It was enough to bring Tom's gun out of his Army-issue holster in less time than it took a man to sneeze. He leveled it at the dark-haired man and said tightly, "If I see that shoulder so much as shiver again, I'm going to blow your brains out the back of your head."

Out of the corner of his eye he saw the standing man's hand drift toward the revolver on his hip. In a flash of movement, Tom brought the butt of his revolver against the side of the man's head. The man cried painfully and fell, turning over a table and two chairs. He lay there moaning and holding his shoulder as Tom returned the barrel of his Army Colt to the man across the table.

"Now me and this lady are going to walk out of here. And if any of you so much as twitch, it'll be the last time."

The three sitting men stared at him. The man on the floor groaned and curled his knees to his chest.

"Mrs. McCrae," Tom said. He could sense her standing behind him.

"Yes," she said after a moment's hesitation. He could hear the fear in her voice.

Glynette's Corporal

"Go outside and bring our horses up to the porch."

He heard her footsteps, the door open, and close. When he heard the clomp of the horses' hooves, he backed to the door. Reaching it, he slid his eyes to Ralph, who stood behind the bar looking wary. Tom stuck a hand in his pocket and tossed Anderson a coin.

"That about cover the meal, Ralph?"

Anderson glanced at the coin. "I'll say it does."

"We'll be seein' you then."

"See you, Tom."

Tom backed through the door. On the porch he turned. Glynette was mounted and holding his horse's reins. The rain had stopped and the clouds were breaking. Red-winged blackbirds sang in the cattails behind the corral. Tom moved down the steps, took the reins from Glynette, and climbed into the leather. "Let's ride."

Chapter Five

They galloped down the road for a half mile, putting distance between themselves and the roadhouse. Tom turned several times to keep an eye on their rear. Finally he shouted, "I don't think they're following us!" and dropped his horse to a canter.

Turning for one last look, he slowed to a walk. "Turn here." They cut between two low rounded buttes, gradual undulations, spreading away from the Antelope Mountains, then angled behind one of the buttes until they could no longer be seen from the road. Tom reined up and listened for hoofbeats.

Glynette sat beside him, trying to keep her breathing quiet. Her heart was throbbing as though it would come though her chest, and she was so breathless she was almost panting. But as she sat, listening and waiting, she realized that her breathlessness was less from fear than exhilaration. It was irrational, she knew, but she was not afraid. She had an implicit faith that Tom would get them through safely. Her eyes were bright, and a faint smile played about her lips. She was not sorry it had happened.

She had never been in a situation as remotely daring as this. It was the stuff dime novels were made of.

Tom began to feel the tightness in his jaw loosen. The hardcases must have stayed at the roadhouse. He sat back in his saddle and released his held breath. Maybe Ralph settled them down, persuaded them to stay with another round of beers and some of his corny joking. They were probably just bored, frustrated, out-of-work cowboys releasing some tension in their own rough way.

He sighed deeply, turned to Glynette and did a double-take. Seeing the little smile playing about her lips, his own lips parted in an incredulous grin. "Ain't you scared?"

She released her breath in a nervous gasp. "A little, I guess."

He chuckled. "Well, you could've fooled me. You still feel like headin' to the ranch, or have you had enough excitement for one day?"

She looked surprised at the question. "Why, of course we're still going to the ranch. I wouldn't dream of disappointing Mr. Demmer." She lifted her chin in the direction of the roadhouse. "Besides, if I let a bunch of uncivilized ruffians like that change my plans, I'd feel as though they had . . . won."

He shook his head admiringly, then gave a casual salute. "Demmer's ranch it is, Captain McCrae."

He and Glynette picked a path in the direction of Demmer's ranch, following the gradual ascent toward the mountain foothills. Soon the last of the clouds disappeared beyond the eastern horizon. The sun shone as warmly as it had the day before, drying out their clothes, sparkling on the rain drops clinging to the prairie grass, and inspiring the meadow larks to resume their song. By the time Demmer's ranch came into view, the rain, the roadhouse, and the ruffians they had encountered there seemed as distant as the clouds scuttling hurriedly to the east.

As Tom and Glynette told Dem, Will, and Arne all about their misadventure at the roadhouse, Dem beamed proudly over what he saw as Tom's latest feat of heroism. Later, Tom helped Dem with his ornery bronc while Glynette strolled lazily through the meadows lining the creek, dreaming and picking wildflowers.

She chatted with Will and his brother Arne while they worked with the young horses, training them to the halter, and getting them used to being touched and brushed and having their feet lifted. She learned that the boys lived on a nearby ranch. The boys' parents, the Stindahls, were Norwegian immigrants who had come with one newborn son to America seventeen years ago, before Will and Arne had been born. The couple had been blessed with ten more sons and, having more than enough to run their own ranch, sent Will and Arne to work for Demmer.

"Doesn't your mother wish she had just one girl?" Glynette asked the boys, amused.

"Oh, ya," Arne answered, "she says if next one is a boy, it haf to wear dresses anyway."

The boys giggled.

"*Next* one?" Glynette asked.

"Ya, baby come soon."

The boys blushed and giggled, and Glynette laughed with them, feeling both sympathy and envy for the overburdened Mrs. Stindahl. The boys were such attractive children, so friendly and polite. She wondered how it would be to raise such fine boys out here in the Montana countryside and watch them grow into proud, strong young men.

When the sun began dropping toward the western hori-

Glynette's Corporal

zon, Tom sauntered over to where Glynette clung to the corral boards watching the boys work, and asked if she was ready to head back to the fort. She said no and smiled. The two visits to the ranch had been the happiest times by far since she had come to Montana, possibly the happiest in her life. She felt at ease here, away from the prying eyes of the fort ladies, away from Anniston and his rules, and the officers assigned to guard her in Anniston's stead.

She felt she could do anything she wanted at the ranch, and no one would be scandalized. If she decided to hike a leg up on the porch railing and smoke a cigar, the two men would be surprised, no doubt, but Mr. Demmer would finally just be amused and Tom would shake his head and salute. Will and Arne would giggle and blush. But no one would try to stop her, no one would flush with anger and shame, no one would give her a lecture on propriety or accuse her of destroying his reputation. She sighed deeply. Indeed she was not ready to head back to the fort. She liked it here just fine.

Tom, also sorry the day was done, pointed out that it was getting late. He was right, of course. She knew as well as he that they must ride into the fort well before retreat to avoid arousing concern from the officers, curiosity from the ladies, and a barrage of questions from both that neither she nor Tom would want to face. Reluctantly they waved good-bye to Demmer, Will, and Arne, and turned their mounts toward Fort Reynolds.

Tom and Glynette were crossing a bowl between a high, rocky crag and a low ridge studded with rocks and cedars when a shot rang out, and Tom's horse gave a start, screaming and bucking before going down on its knees. Another shot sounded as Tom jumped off the thrashing horse before it rolled on top of him. Glynette's horse was crow-stepping, startled, as she struggled to control him.

"What's happening?" she said.

A lead slug spanged off a rock only a foot to Glynette's left. "Someone's shooting at us! Get down!" Tom reached for his rifle and stopped. The dying horse was lying on it. Cursing and turning toward Glynette, Tom reached up, grabbed her around the waist, and pulled her from the saddle. He set her down and took her hand. "Come on!"

Hand in hand, guns popping behind them, slugs thumping the ground around them, they ran to the low ridge, scrambled over the rocks, and hunkered down. Unholstering his revolver, Tom peered between a large, lichen-flecked rock and a small, wind-twisted cedar at the rocky-topped butte about two hundred yards away. Smoke puffed among the talus and rocks and ponderosa pines.

"Keep your head down," Tom said. "They're above us, and they have rifles."

"Who's *they*?" Glynette cried.

"Our friends from the roadhouse. They must've waited here to drygulch us on our way back to the fort."

"What do you mean, 'drygulch?'"

"Ambush. Bushwhack. Trap." Tom swiped sweat from his brow. "They killed my horse."

"What are we going to do?"

Tom looked around behind them. The ground sloped gently away to Elk Creek, about a quarter mile away. They could make a run for it, but there was no cover between here and the creek. The hardcases would only run them down, probably backshoot Tom and take Mrs. McCrae. The thought of what they'd do to her sent a chill up his spine.

"I reckon we wait here. There's nowhere to go. I'll try to hold them off with my six-shooter. Maybe they'll get bored with their little game and decide to hightail it back to their camp and whiskey bottles." He thought what had probably saved them so far was the men's inebriation and inability to shoot straight.

Glynette hunkered next to Tom, peering through the rocks at the ridge above them, where smoke still puffed and rifles cracked. "What do they *want*?" she implored.

The answer appeared to dawn on Glynette as her eyes met Tom's. Her eyes widened momentarily. Then she turned, sitting on her butt, her back to a cedar root and the rock ridge.

"Don't worry, Mrs. McCrae, they're not going to get you."

Something caught her eye, and her eyes turned dark. "Tom, what's that?" She pointed to the damp redness on the side of his coat, under his left arm.

"Just a little blood. They grazed me, is all."

Glynette gave a choked sob, her eyes filled with a terrified awe.

"Just a burn," Tom said.

"You're bleeding."

"That's good. It'll keep the poison out."

Glynette's eyes sought his again, bright with terror. Tears glistened in them. "Oh, Tom . . . what are we going to do?"

She feared more for him now than for herself. The blood-soaked tunic was an appalling reminder of his mortality—Tom, the fearless soldier with whom she'd felt so safe. Tom could die. She wanted to throw herself against him, wrap her arms around him, feel his bulk against her, warm and alive.

"Shhh . . ." He suddenly dropped his head, lay flat against the ground, and lifted his chin to peer just over the tops of the rocks. "Someone's coming."

Tom sent his gaze northward, toward the bottom of the butte, where he'd just seen a flash of movement. There was a rise to his right. Someone was behind that rise, making his way closer to Tom and Glynette. He'd no sooner thought it than a head and rifle appeared in the grass about fifty yards away, a blue bandanna ruffling in the breeze. Smoke puffed around the rifle, and the slug pinged off a rock several feet to Tom's left.

"Come on out boys and girls!" the man yelled in a taunting sing-song voice. "It's play time."

Glynette felt a spurt of panic biting into her chest. She flattened herself against the rocks, wide-eyed with fear. Tom raised his pistol, took aim, and squeezed the trigger. The shot landed several feet before the rifleman, who fired again, smoke puffing around his head. This time the man's slug was so close that Tom felt the sting of rock and lead fragments in his face. He swore under his breath.

He steadied his hand on the army Colt, using a rock as a rest, squinting down the barrel. He squeezed the trigger. The gun jumped. A red spot appeared on the neck of the rifleman, and Tom heard a muffled cry. The man turned onto his side and froze.

Glimpsing a blur of color out of the corner of his left eye, Tom turned. He heard a whoop and saw a man galloping a horse up the grade, materializing out of the brome and wheat grass. The man held a pistol in each hand, his reins in his teeth. The brim of his dirty tan Stetson blew flat against his forehead. Smoke puffed from his guns.

"Keep your head down!" Cajoling himself to remain calm, Tom took a knee, and clamped his left hand to the wrist of his right as he leveled the Colt. The gun barked, once, twice, three times. The horse whinnied and raised up on its hind legs as the man somersaulted backward off the saddle. He lay in the grass, groaning, and Tom brought the Colt to bear again and finished him. The horse turned in a wide circle, and headed back in the direction it had come.

Another burst of rifle fire lifted from the butte top, the lead buzzing around Tom's ears like autumn blackflies. Instinctively, he grabbed his throat, gave a yell, and tumbled back behind the rocks.

Glynette screamed and bolted toward him, taking his head in her hands. His neck was limp. "No, no," she moaned, "you can't be dead!"

Tom glanced sideways and winked. "I'm not." He held his index finger to his lips, signaling her for silence.

Glynette's despair turned to ecstatic relief. Crying silently, she threw her arms around the soldier's neck and hugged him. "Oh, Tom . . . I thought—"

"Shh. Hopefully they thought so too." He stroked her hair, then closed his eyes tightly and pushed her away. He climbed to a sitting position well below the lip of the ridge, and began reloading his revolver from the cartridge pouch on his belt. "If they think I'm dead and you're all alone, the other two might decide to come on over for a visit."

"How could that possibly be desirable?" Glynette said with a shudder, wiping tears from her cheeks.

"Then they won't wait until after dark. They'll come now, and I can kill them."

Glynette winced at the baldness of the statement.

Tom closed his gun and spun the cylinder. He looked at her. "I know it sounds cold, but those are cold men. It's us or them."

Glynette nodded, pressing her lips together.

"You sit down there a ways," Tom said, "well down from the rocks. That way, if they come over the rocks, the first thing they'll see is you, and they'll forget all about me."

Tom lay parallel to the ridge, hunkered close against the rocks. Glynette sat about ten yards below him, her knees hugged to her chest, wisps of loose hair blowing in the wind. They sat like that for fifteen minutes. Then they heard voices. A horse whinnied.

"Honey . . . you all alone over there?" a man asked.

Tom figured he was about fifty yards away. He didn't want to lift his head over the rocks and give himself away. The man had to be closer before he dared fire a shot. If the men thought he was still alive and waiting for them, they'd probably disappear and wait for dark to storm Tom and Glynette, when the odds would be in their favor.

"Hey, sweety sugar," the man called again, his voice shrill with mockery. "The soldier boy done gone to meet the great general in the sky?"

Tom said in a stage whisper, "Tell them to leave you alone."

A moment passed and Glynette cried loudly, her voice cracking with genuine fear, "Leave me alone!"

The man laughed. His laughter was joined by another.

"You wait here," the first man said.

Behind the rocks, Tom thumbed back the hammer of his revolver and steadied his breathing, staring unseeingly at a spider crawling up out of a hole in the rocky ground beneath him. He hoped both men would come at once, together.

After a minute, which seemed like an hour, Tom heard boots crunching grass and the raspy sound of a man breathing—a man unused to walking. The sounds stopped.

"Missy, you over there?" The man's voice had lost its mockery. It owned a wary edge now.

Tom heard the metallic, scraping sound of a bullet being levered into a rifle breech. The sound of boots crunching grass resumed, as did the breathing. They grew louder, clearer, until . . .

"Honey, girl . . . hee-hee . . . Daddy's home!"

Tom jerked himself onto his knees. The dark-haired man with the black mustache and red bandanna stood about twenty feet away, just on the other side of the rocky ridge, staring down at Glynette. His eyes were bright with laughter. Stepping toward Glynette with a leer, he saw Tom in the periphery of his vision. His smile dropped, and he jerked around, facing Tom, bringing the rifle down to his waist.

Before he could fire, Tom lifted the revolver and shot the man in the forehead. The rifle barked as the man fell backward, the round sailing skyward, and he lay dead, a hole the size of a penny filling with blood between his eyes.

Glynette gasped and flung herself face down.

Tom jerked around to face the other man, about a hundred yards away. The man was backing up, clinging to the reins of both horses. Finally, he turned, mounted one of the horses, and rode away, trailing the second horse behind him. Tom dropped his gun to his side, letting the man go. He knew the man's retreat was for real; with his companions dead and the odds no longer in his favor, he'd be long out of the country in a couple hours.

Tom looked up to see Glynette standing beside him, staring down at the dead man.

"It's over," Tom told her. "At least as far as the cutthroats go. We still have to find a way back to the fort."

Glynette tore her eyes from the dead man, dragging her thoughts away as well. "My horse . . ."

"Long gone," Tom said, scanning the horizon. "All that shooting." He looked down the grade at his own horse lying dead in the blond grass. "And mine's coyote food. We've got to get out of here." He rose to his knees and tried to stand, but stumbled, his vision swimming, and sank back down against the rocks. Blood dripped from the bottom of his coat onto the ground.

"Tom," Glynette gasped, rushing to his side. She pushed her arm under his shoulder and clutched him as best she could, avoiding the wound in his side. She eased him to a half-reclined position against the rocks. "We've got to stop the bleeding."

He nodded weakly, dismayed to find that now the adreneline rush of the ambush was passed, his strength was fading. He was too weak too stand, yet he had to walk. They had to get back to the fort. Mindlessly, he again put his hands against the rock and tried again to push himself up.

"Tom, what are you doing?" Glynette pushed him down by his shoulders against the rocks. He was pale, and a sheen of sweat glistened on his face. "We have to get you out of that coat," she said, grasping the brass buttons and working them one by one. When the coat fell open, she grabbed the lapels and pulled him forward, working her way behind him to keep him propped up.

"You have to get your arms out of the sleeves, Tom. Can you do that?" She was trying to keep her voice calm, though she felt a rising panic as she saw the challenge of simply extracting him from his coat.

Tom steeled himself and pulled his shoulders and arms back. The moment he did, a burning sear jolted through his left rib cage, and he involuntarily pulled forward again. But it had been enough for her to peel the coat back from his shoulders and begin tugging it loose from the right arm. He bent the arm as best he could to help, and once the right arm was finally free, she was able to pull

Glynette's Corporal

the entire coat away without any further jarring. Tom lay back with a groan.

Hurriedly she fumbled with the buttons of his shirt. Tears filled her eyes as she worked, and her mind filled with a steady chant—"Oh God, oh God, please don't die, oh God, please don't die"—blocking out all other thought.

When the shirt was unbuttoned, she clapped a hand over her mouth and suppressed a gasp.

"Use my shirt to bind the wound," Tom said.

They struggled him out of his shirt, and she quickly twisted the blood-soaked cloth. "You'll have to sit up again so I can get this around you."

"Wait," he groaned. "Look at my back . . . make sure the bullet went through." He made a struggling motion to turn over. She moved to his side and lifted, pushing him up enough to see the area on his back that was opposite the hole in the front. His back was smeared with blood and coated with dirt and pebbles, but the exit hole was clearly there.

"Good, that's good." He smiled weakly, as he eased himself back down.

"I'm going down to get the canteen," Glynette said. She scanned the horizon. Even though she knew the last man was long gone, she was still uneasy leaving the safety of Tom's side.

"You want my gun?"

"I don't know how to use it, remember?"

He frowned. "We'll have to work on that."

She hurried down the rocky bank and across to where Tom's horse had fallen. She lifted the canteen as well as Tom's knapsack, thankful they weren't crushed beneath the horse.

As she knelt beside Tom and pulled the stopper from

the canteen, he stirred and said, "You should know how to use a gun."

"Shhh," she said softly, but smiled.

She examined the cloth over the wound. The bleeding had slowed considerably. She uncorked the canteen and helped him hold it. He drank greedily, and the water seemed to revive him some.

"Mrs. McCrae," he gasped, "I'm sorry I brought you out here. I—"

She touched her fingers to his lips. "Don't, Tom. Please don't insult me by saying you're sorry. I was the one who wanted to come out here. I'm the one who should be sorry. You're shot and your horse is dead, and you're probably going to be in trouble because the commanding officer is going to want to know why *you* brought helpless little *me* out here." She snorted in disgust and made a move to rise. "So I don't want to hear any more about sorry."

"Wait," Tom said, putting a hand on her arm. "I just want you to know . . . I'm sorry, anyway."

"Go ahead . . . eat your heart out with guilt if you want, but I wouldn't take anything for the last two days. They've been the best of my life . . . except for the part where you get shot." She picked up the canteen. "Drink some more water."

He kept his eyes on her face as he drank, and when she lowered the canteen, he wiped his mouth with one hand and smiled. "You make a fine nurse, Mrs. McCrae."

"Well, you're my first patient, so I'm glad you're not particular." She was relieved to see him smile. He looked better.

She looked around them, wondering how they would ever get out of here. The rayless red ball of the sun dropped toward the horizon. Almost retreat. As a striker,

Glynette's Corporal

Tom didn't have to report to roll call. How long would it take until someone noticed they were missing?

"Will they send someone to look for us tonight?"

"Probably," he said, "but it isn't likely they'll find us. We're too far off the trail. Rescue details would have to stick to the main trails until daylight." He gave her a firm, reassuring look. "We'll make it. Don't worry."

Glynette stared in the direction of the fort. "We're only a few miles from the post. I could get there in a couple of hours and . . ."

He shook his head vigorously. "No. It'll be dark soon. You won't know the way. It's safer to wait until daylight. They'll come for us."

She squinted into the light of the setting sun. He was right. She would rather face being stranded out here than to begin a lonely walk over that vast landscape where the last of the cutthroats might be waiting for a final ambush to avenge his friends.

She leaned over him to inspect the bandage. The pressure of the wrap seemed to be working. Very little fresh blood seeped through the cloth. She looked around, her eyes lighting on a grassy area just below them. "We should move you down there where it's softer, and you'll be out of that pool of blood."

She pushed herself under his arm again and lifted, but once on his feet, he seemed much stronger. He staggered to the place she had indicated without her help, eased himself to the ground there, and lay back again. She followed him with the canteen.

"Good. Now we can clean you up a bit."

She tipped the canteen over him and washed away some of the smeared, dried blood from around his shoulders and neck with her hand. She touched him softly, watching her own pale, slender fingers slide against his tanned, muscular neck and shoulders.

Her eyes lingered on his broad, deep-muscled chest lightly covered with auburn hair, then trailed down the line of hair from his chest to his taut, flat belly, her eyes stopping where the hair disappeared beneath his pants. Her lips parted and her breath came shallowly. She wanted to lie against his chest and belly and have his arms around her.

She lifted her eyes, and they met his. He had seen her staring at him. He looked at her with the understanding of a man who desires a woman that desires him. "Here," he said huskily, holding out his hand. "You have blood on your face. Pour some water in my hand."

She tipped the canteen and poured a little water onto his palm.

"Lean toward me," he said.

She leaned forward, her eyes still on his. He wiped her cheek with his wet hand. Feeling the caress of his hand on her face, she dropped her eyes and unconsciously tilted her cheek against his hand.

"More," he said, taking his hand away and holding it out again.

She swallowed, ran her tongue over her lips, and tilted the canteen over his hand again. Then she sat still, her eyes averted as he stroked her face again, breathing in short shallow breaths.

He turned his hand to the dry backside, and smoothed the water away from her face. He did it gently, his eyes never leaving her face. He moved the hand into a cup at the nape of her neck beneath her hair. She leaned her head into the hand, her eyes growing smoky. Her lips parted softly, and she leaned down to him, her lips only inches from his. She swam in the greenness of his eyes, the warmth of his gaze, then leaned against him and pressed her mouth to his.

For a moment he returned the kiss, pressing his mouth

to hers, before coming to his senses and pushing her gently away. It felt like the hardest thing he'd ever done. He lay back and gazed at her, his hand still on the nape of her neck. His face had an intensity that sent tremors through her almost as violent as the kiss had, for she understood what it meant. In the moment of that kiss, something had changed between them. Something that until now they had both desperately ignored suddenly exploded into the open, refusing to be denied any longer.

She felt light-headed, and suddenly the world she knew was lost to her. As she looked around, everything looked strange. The pebbles cast impossibly long shadows in the last light. An unearthly red light set their skin and hair afire. They were all that existed, a man and a woman, afloat on a sea of sun-blazened prairie grass, with no history, no identities. All the barriers had been broken. The old roles didn't fit. Suddenly she could not conceive of herself as the wife of Captain Anniston McCrae or Tom as the soldier hired to serve her. The fort, their lives, everything seemed to exist in some distant memory, in some other universe.

The sun dropped behind the western hills, and the red glow that had tinged everything retreated into soft shadows of blue and green. When the sun disappeared, the spell was broken. Glynette shivered in the chill air. When she turned back to Tom, she could see that time had started again for him too.

Now what would they do? He leaned up suddenly and looked deeply into her eyes, as if to draw her back. He smiled. "We should make a camp."

"All right," she said, though she had no idea what he meant. How could they make a camp? With what? They had no tent, no cooking utensils, no food to cook.

He turned his head toward Elk Creek. "We'll go down by the creek. We can gather wood there and build a fire."

"Can you make it that far?" she asked, uncertain. Although the creek was maybe a quarter mile away, it seemed too far.

He struggled to his feet before she could help him up. "It's gonna get awful cold if we stay here, and we don't want to be in the open." He leaned down to pick up his coat and canteen, but a sharp pain to his left side forced him to straighten.

"I'll get everything," Glynette scolded. "Please don't make any unnecessary movements, or you'll start bleeding again."

"Yes, ma'am. In that case, you might want to pull the saddle blanket off my horse too."

Slowly they traversed the space between them and the tree-lined banks of the creek, then followed a deer trail into the underbrush. The only sound was that of rippling waters and a single song bird.

"This looks like a fine spot here," he said, indicating the level, grassy area where they stood.

It's perfect," Glynette agreed, looking around at the clearing matted here and there with soft leaves.

Tom sat with a groan next to the creek, drained from the exertion and, looking up at her apologetically, said, "I'll need you to help gather some wood. I don't think I'll be able to do it all myself."

She gave him an exasperated look. "*I'll* do it all. You rest." She set his coat, canteen, blanket and knapsack next to him on the ground. "Just tell me what to do."

"Bring leaves and twigs to get it started. I'll just rest a minute." He fell back with a sigh.

Glynette found plenty of leaves nearby, for they were under a stand of burr oaks. After gathering several dry handfuls and piling them near where Tom lay, she wandered off to forage for twigs. In no time she had an armful, which she deposited next to the pile of leaves and Tom, who appeared now to be sleeping.

She knelt beside him. She had never seen him asleep before. He looked peaceful, his right hand tucked under his head, his features still. His chest rose and fell in deep, even breaths. She wanted to reach down and stroke his hair, but instead she picked up the saddle blanket where it lay in a heap beside him and spread it lightly over him, then returned to her work.

She found a dead, fallen tree from which she gathered branch after branch of perfectly dry, seasoned wood, and several aspen branches which she dragged back to add to her growing pile. She worked with a single-minded concentration, strangely happy in what might be considered dire circumstances, and soon, by her own estimation, her pile was monstrous. As she dragged back an oak log so heavy she could barely tug it through the grass and tangled undergrowth, Tom sat up suddenly and looked around, hand hovering near his holster.

"It's just me," she said.

He pushed the blanket aside and shook his head. "I fell asleep." Then in the twilight, he caught sight of the stacks of branches surrounding him. He threw back his head and laughed.

"Good heavens, woman," he exclaimed, with a look that said he was impressed. "I didn't know you had it in you."

Dropping the log at the edge of the clearing, she beamed, feeling silly to be so proud of a stack of dead wood, but feeling that its presence proved something about her to him. Perhaps she was stronger than he thought—or than she thought. She recalled with pride that she had not cried or screamed while she and Tom were under fire; she had not lost her mind with fear. And now she had shown she was not afraid to work, not afraid to get her hands dirty.

She fished around in his knapsack and pulled out a box of matches. He kept his eyes on her dark form, as the blues and greens of dusk faded into the deep, mysterious indigo of night.

"You're a fine woman, Mrs. McCrae," he said quietly, "not bad to have along when the chips are down."

It was so dark now, she could see only his silhouette and the faint shine of his eyes in the fading light. "I reckon you might as well call me Glynette."

"Glynette," he whispered. He spread his coat for her. "You sit down and rest now. I'll build a fire."

Soon the dry leaves and twigs crackled and a golden circle of light surrounded them. The warmth felt good, for though the day had been unusually hot, the night air grew chill. Glynette sat with her arms around her knees and watched worriedly as Tom continued to break branches into lengths. His jaw tightened and he winced as he worked. No longer able to stand it, she said, "Tom, that's enough. You're going to open that wound."

He dropped the pieces he'd just broken on the stack and groaned. "I think you're right, boss."

He sat down beside her with a sigh, and they stared into the flames, both of them settling into the strange little universe of flickering light they had created.

"I like being out here," Glynette said at length.

"What do you like?"

"Being away from people. Not having to worry about what's proper, only about what needs to be done."

He nodded. "I like the quiet."

She listened, hearing nothing but the light rippling of the creek and the crackling of the fire. "I like the quiet too." She rested her head on her knees and turned her face to him. "I like being with you."

He looked at her with that steady gaze that made her bones go soft, the look of a man who has shed everything but the thought of a woman. She grew uncomfortable under the heat of his gaze and raised her head slightly, but did not avert her eyes.

He cleared his throat and turned away. "I'll bet you're hungry." He dug into his knapsack, producing a paper sack.

She shook her head. Food would only take away the feeling of lightness she had, the sensation of floating beyond the pulls of the earth.

He held the sack in front of her. "You should eat. It's raisins and currants. I've got hard tack too."

"Maybe later."

She leaned back and stared into the fire, and soon felt him relax beside her. "Were you named Glynette after your father?"

"My mother's maiden name. I was supposed to be named Glynn, but when I surprised my parents by being a girl, I was christened with the cumbersome feminine version." She laughed. "I wish they'd just called me Glynn, anyway. It sounds feminine enough, don't you think?"

He chuckled. "Well, it's better than Frank or Bill."

They lay for a while in silence. Then she turned to him, her beautiful, pale face bathed in firelight. "You are the finest, bravest man alive, Tom Flint."

He smiled, staring at her a long time. He resisted the urge to pull her to him. She was so beautiful. He loved her as he would never love another woman . . . yet he would never have her. His heart tightened at the thought, yet he'd lived long enough and suffered enough to know by now that life cared nothing for our dreams and wishes.

"You're pretty brave yourself, Mrs. McCrae."

She matched his smile, meeting his gaze. Then her lips parted.

He knew if he touched her, kissed her, she wouldn't resist. She loved him as he loved her. Fighting the urge to touch her took every bit of his strength, and he almost groaned aloud with the effort. Before he could stop her, she leaned forward and touched her lips to his. He savored the velvety feel of her skin against his. Then, grasping her by the shoulders, he held her back.

She smiled sadly, understanding. He was a man of honor. It was part of what she loved about him. How ironic that it was also what would keep her from having one blissful night in his embrace. She folded her arms across her legs, and they fell into a silence that communicated as deeply as if their souls were merging. Letting the stars roll over, watching the logs soften and collapse and disappear into the dancing flames, each thought of nothing but the other. Each felt the same love and heartbreak consuming them.

They lay awake together until deep in the night, nibbling fruit, talking softly about their childhoods and their dreams, feeding wood to the fire. Their words were sweet and caressing, and each clung to the sound of every syllable the other spoke. Only after the moon had set, and the night had grown deep and still, did they doze a little, snuggling against each other for warmth.

Chapter Six

Glynette awoke with a shiver. In the dim first light, she sat up and saw Tom propped against a log by the fire smoking a cigarette. She looked across the fire at him. He smiled his sad smile and took a drag from his cigarette.

"Guess we'd better get going. They'll be looking for us for sure now." He stood. "I'll step out into the clearing and see if I can see anything."

"Here," she said, "you'll need your coat." She pulled the coat she'd been sleeping on from beneath her and smiled at him vaguely, questioningly, sensing the chasm already forming between them.

Her heart already knew what her brain had not had time to realize. It was ending scarcely before it had begun. What had happened between them would not be spoken of again.

Tom pushed the branches from the path of the deer trail until he stood again on the open prairie, his heart heavy at the thought of what lay ahead of them. Not so much for himself as for Glynette. The curiosity, the questions, the stares, the cruel insinuations of the women, the open lust of the men. A man and a woman alone in the wilds all night—everyone would wonder what had happened between them, and they would scrutinize her ruthlessly for a sign.

"We'll head over to the army road," he said, as they stood in the clearing, adjusting themselves to the morning light, the open space, and the task ahead of them. "It's further to the fort, but we're more likely to be seen and get picked up."

Their thoughts weighted their steps as they walked the nearly two miles to the road, half dreading their rescue. By now, Glynette had begun to realize what was likely in store for them, shuddering as she imagined the onslaught of concern and helpfulness from the officers' wives.

Tom's shoulders sagged with regret as he, too, imagined the bored garrison busybodies making life miserable for Glynette. They would assume she'd had an affair with her striker simply because life was exceedingly dull on a small military outpost, and they would want it to be true. Tom stopped. Grasping Glynette by the shoulders, he turned her to him. "I'm sorry, Glynette . . . Mrs. McCrae. I—"

She pressed her fingers to his lips and smiled sadly. "Don't insult me by saying you're sorry, Tom." She moved her fingertips to trace the line of his jaw wonderingly. "And don't be sorry. Whatever happens will be worth it."

Long before they reached the road, they saw the horses. There were four riders, their blue coats and sabers announcing that they were soldiers, probably one of as many four-man search details as the depleted garrison could spare. When the men spotted them, one raised his pistol in the air and fired three shots, a signal to the other searchers that Mrs. Captain McCrae and Corporal Tom Flint had been found.

"Corporal Flint!" called one of the riders.

Glynette's Corporal

Tom lifted his forage hat in a wave of recognition and said dryly, "Well, Mrs. McCrae, we've been saved."

The four men galloped up in a flurry of dust and hoofbeats, slowing their mounts to a walk for the last twenty yards. When they reined up, the men tipped their hats in deference to Captain McCrae's wife and directed friendly nods and salutes to Tom.

Glynette could sense their shyness in her presence immediately. Had Tom been the sole object of their rescue, the greetings would have been boisterous, full of back-slapping, joking, and crude epithets. The question that was in their minds would have popped out of every mouth, "What in tarnation happened to you?"

Instead, the men sat their mounts stiffly, casting furtive glances at Glynette. She felt acutely self-conscious in her dirty, torn habit, with her hair disheveled. Finally, a thickset redhead who wore the chevron of a corporal dismounted, smiling stiffly. "There's a few people around the post who'll be happy to see the two of you."

He reached out a hand to Tom. "Good to see you, Tom."

Tom grasped the hand. "Likewise, Kerr."

"Looks like you're injured."

Tom nodded and pulled aside his jacket. "Shot clean through. It ain't bad. Reckon we could hitch a ride?"

Kerr handed his reins to Tom. "Take my horse. I'll double with Chaney."

He looked uncertainly at Glynette. "Mrs. McCrae . . . ?"

"Will ride with me," Tom said.

"Right," Kerr said, glancing at the other men.

While the single riders rode ahead to report to the commanding officer and announce to the anxious garrison that Tom and Mrs. McCrae were safe, the double riders walked their mounts. Along the way, Tom told Kerr and Chaney about their misadventures with the four cutthroats.

Glynette held Tom's waist loosely as they rode, her face

turned away from the soldiers. She resisted the urge to wrap her arms around him and press her cheek to his back. The rhythmic swaying of the horse, the ground passing before her eyes, the smells of sage and horse, absorbed her attention wholly, her mind being too overwhelmed for thought. She was startled when they reached the fort. She looked up to see sentries and men on fatigue forgetting their jobs to stare at them, then Captain Sherry striding across the grounds from headquarters, and ladies spilling onto their porches. She tightened her hold on Tom.

"It'll be okay," he whispered.

Tom reined up before headquarters and saluted as Captain Sherry met them. Sherry did not return the salute. He stared coldly at Glynette.

"Mrs. McCrae," he all but shouted, "you certainly did give us a scare. Can you walk? Do you need an ambulance brought?"

"No, Captain, I'm quite all right." She felt irritated at his tone, so like Anniston's, as though he was admonishing a naughty child.

Tom dismounted and turned to give her a hand. Captain Sherry nudged him out of the way.

"Take my hand," he said brusquely.

Glynette obeyed the command and stepped to the ground.

"Come, I'll take you to the hospital." Captain Sherry held out his arm.

"I don't need the surgeon." She ignored the arm. "Really, Captain, I'm quite all right. It's Tom who is in need of medical attention."

Sherry cast an accusing glance at Tom. "You'll need to report to headquarters first, Mr. Flint."

"Yes, sir."

"Captain Sherry," Glynette protested, "he's been . . ."

Tom gave her an urgent look that made her stop mid-sentence. She understood. Tom would have to do it their way. She fumed at the absurdity, the injustice of it. Captain Sherry trying to force her to the hospital though she had no injury, and poor Tom with a bullet hole made to stand in the fusty office of headquarters and endure what was sure to be a grueling question and answer.

She sighed. "I am very tired, Mr. Sherry, so unless you would like to detain me for questioning also, I think I will go to my quarters and lie down."

He narrowed his eyes at her, not missing the acidity of her tone. "If you are quite sure you are not in need of medical attention, Mrs. McCrae . . ." His look was probing, insinuating.

Lifting her chin, she mustered what dignity she could with her loose hair flying about her face, her clothes torn, dirty, and covered with blood. "Quite sure."

She turned on her heel, only to face Lucy Britzman, Sibyl Nye, and Dinah Sherry in a small pack blocking the path. She cut her eyes down the row of officers' quarters. In the nearby duplexes, officer's wives leaned against the railing, straining to catch every word; others had left their porches to inch slowly down the walk in the direction of headquarters, their eyes glued to Glynette.

Glynette hesitated before this hoard of women, then took a tentative step forward. It was enough to set the pack in motion, Lucy leading the way.

"You poor dear! What happened?" the women cried in a chorus, surrounding her.

"Come inside," Lucy commanded, tugging her toward the steps. "I'll get you a cup of hot tea and some food."

"Please." Glynette attempted to sidestep them. "I appreciate your concern, but I really must lie down. I'm quite worn out."

"Well, of course you are . . ." Sibyl said, blocking Glynette's path.

"You can rest at my house," Lucy said. "You mustn't be alone after what you've been through."

Glynette shook her head, an absolute negative. "Thank you for your concern, but no."

"Mrs. McCrae, please," Dinah said, with a look of perplexity to the others. The women were bursting to know what had happened, but the silly girl was not cooperating. "Let us assist you."

"Your house has had no fire," Sibyl added, falling in beside her and urging her forward. "The morning chill will make you sick."

"I won't hear another word," Lucy said. She boldly fell in on the other side and tugged Glynette forward. "Anniston would be appalled if we left you alone at a time like this."

Glynette had literally dug in her heels and was quite resolved not to budge, but hearing Anniston's name employed as an excuse for their demands brought home the hopelessness of her position. The ladies had not only the sanction of their own self-deluded sense of virtue to justify their charade, but that of Anniston, acting commander Captain Sherry, and by extension, all of society.

"Glynette!" a voice cried.

Glynette's head jerked up. Maggie! It was Maggie rushing down the gravel walk. Glynette tore away from the women and fell into Maggie's arms.

"Get rid of them," Glynette whispered.

Maggie stared at the women, lips pressed together, disgusted. Then she said in a genteel tone that no one could find fault with, "Don't you ladies worry. I'll take care of Mrs. McCrae."

Glynette and Maggie turned and started down the walk. The ladies were dumbfounded. Their prize had just been stolen from them, and all they could do was watch hungrily.

"Let me know if you need anything," Sibyl called. "I'll drop by in a bit to see how you're faring."

Lucy scowled at Sibyl. "I'll drop by in a while, too, dear," she said firmly.

Maggie slammed the door on the sound of their voices. "Busybodies," she grumbled.

Glynette entered Maggie's parlor with a sigh of relief. Neddie was there in his usual place on his alphabet quilt, rolling a wagon back and forth and making small unintelligible sounds of delight. "Hey, sweetkins." She smoothed a hand over his downy head.

"Gan!" he cried, still unable to say her name.

Maggie disappeared into the kitchen then returned to the parlor to find her dirty, disheveled friend settled into an arm chair with Ned crawling onto her lap.

She swooped Ned up and said, "Glynette has to rest, Neddie. She isn't well. You play quietly in the floor."

Ned scowled and bunched his face as though he would howl a protest, but he stared at Glynette and, sensing that he would not get much fun from her today, allowed himself to be deposited on his quilt and again turned his attention to his wagon.

"Lie on the davenport," Maggie ordered.

"No, Maggie, I might fall asleep, and you'll need to lie here yourself. I'm comfortable."

"You lie down. That's an order. Joe is bringing you something to eat."

Glynette stretched on the davenport, and Maggie kneeled on the floor beside her, stroking her hair.

"Now, tell me what you need, dear," she said gently. "Do you want to go to sleep after you eat? Or do you want a bath?"

"I want to sleep," Glynette said, her eyes already drooping.

Maggie fetched an afghan from the back of the chair,

spread it over Glynette, and returned to her position by Glynette's side.

Glynette's heart swelled with gratitude. "You're a dear, Maggie."

Before she fell asleep she told Maggie about the rain storm, the ruffians at the roadhouse, and the ambush. She stopped suddenly, however, after saying, "So we had to make a camp at the creek." Glynette's look became pensive and she fell silent.

Maggie wondered at her sudden lapse into introspection, then instinctively sensed the truth. "You're in love with Tom."

Glynette shook her head and closed her eyes. "Nothing happened."

"That's not what I said," Maggie said knowingly.

Tom stood before the broad mahogany desk of the commanding officer, his forage cap held loosely in front of him, his eyes on the map of Montana Territory behind the desk. A visit to headquarters was a rare experience for him, but over the years the office never seemed to change. There were still no curtains on the windows, no carpets on the warped pine floors, and other than unframed maps of the United States, the division of the Missouri, and the department of Dakota, nothing adorned the dun-colored walls.

Acting commander Captain Sherry sat behind the desk lighting a cigar, slowly turning the cylinder between his fingers and puffing, considering the story Tom had just told him. Tom wondered if the man was sober. It was said that in the years Captain Sherry had been at Fort Reynolds he had not once been cold sober. Tom wasn't particularly surprised that his fate was being considered by a drunk. Many of the commanding officers drank too much. Exiled to this lonely, frozen outpost, they used alcohol to keep from going loco.

After puffing the cigar thoughtfully for a moment, Sherry turned to the orderly who sat at a small adjacent desk furiously scribbling notes. "Order a four-man detail from G to confiscate the bodies of the men Corporal Flint purportedly shot."

Then he sat back, puffing his cigar and eyeing Tom dubiously. The orderly pulled a fresh sheet of paper, wrote several lines, and slid the paper in front of Captain Sherry who signed it and pushed it away. The orderly opened the door to the antecroom, thrust the paper at a clerk, then returned to his desk and picked up his pen expectantly.

At length Captain Sherry sighed and said, "What I'm really interested in knowing, Mr. Flint, is what you were doing taking Mrs. McCrae to Demmer's Ranch in the first place."

"She asked to go."

Sherry pulled his cigar from his mouth and looked at Tom as if he were a fool. "Good God, man, that's ten miles away. What were you thinking?"

Tom knew there was no satisfactory answer to the question. He had ridden to Demmer's Ranch for seven years now without incident and had lost his sense of how dangerous it could be.

Sherry studied the end of his cigar. "Did Captain McCrae ask you to take his wife there?"

"He asked me to take her riding, sir."

Sherry's eyes bulged with incredulity, and he bellowed, "Did he know you meant to take her to a ranch outside the protection of the reserve, with no other women about?"

Tom met the man's gaze. "We didn't discuss it."

"Do you have any idea how delicate a lady's reputation

is, Corporal? Do you understand how an incident like this can tarnish her image?" He said it as though he knew quite well that Tom, an enlisted man, hadn't an inkling what he meant. He didn't wait for an answer. "If Captain McCrae were here, he would dismiss you from his employ and request a court-martial. In his stead, I will do both."

Tom's features remained impassive. His regret at endangering Glynette had little to do with a court-martial or anything Captain Sherry could do to him.

"Have you nothing to say for yourself?"

"No, sir."

"Mr. Flint, you are under arrest," the captain said with scarcely contained disgust. "Relieve yourself of your weapon and report to the hospital. When the surgeon releases you, you will be taken to the guard house."

Glynette sat in the dark dining room of her quarters feeding Kola a handful of oats and wondering what to do. It was late, and Tom wasn't home. She assumed the surgeon had kept him at the hospital.

She had slept all day at Maggie's, not awakening until retreat. Then she had picked her way home through the backyards to avoid the officers' wives who had been hunting in ones and twos all day. All day they had taken turns knocking on Maggie's door to inquire about Glynette's condition. Then they would congregate on each other's porches to share the scant morsels of gossip gleaned from the tight-lipped Maggie.

Glynette set Kola on the floor, saying, "That's all for now, fat boy." She had to find out what had happened to Tom. She washed up, changed clothes, brushed and braided her hair, then walked quickly to the hospital at the end of the parade.

When she entered the hospital's anteroom, the orderly,

a middle-aged man with full, wet lips and heavy bags under his eyes, looked up from his newspaper and stared at her in astonishment. A young pimply faced soldier with a sickly row of whiskers across his upper lip sat in a straightback chair against the wall. He stood up and threw his shoulders back.

Glynette approached the orderly's desk. "I'm Mrs. Captain Anniston McCrae. I am looking for my striker, Corporal Thomas Flint."

The orderly cut his eyes to the young soldier, who hesitated, weighing the authority of the post commander against that of a lady. "Five minutes," he said, a pleading note in his voice. "He's not supposed to have *any* visitors."

The orderly led her through the doorway of the hospital ward. Most of the cots were empty, except for one boyish-looking young man reading a magazine and Tom, who sat on his cot playing solitaire, the cards spread on the bed before him. The orderly nodded in Tom's direction, then turned and shuffled back up the aisle.

Tom lifted his head as Glynette approached. He looked exhausted and not at all happy to see her. "Tom . . . what is going on? Why is there a guard posted at the door?"

He flipped another card. "To make sure I don't escape." He tossed a three of hearts onto a four of spades. "You shouldn't have come here," he said gently.

Glynette glanced at the boy on the cot across from Tom. He jerked his magazine back up to his face. Glynette turned back to Tom.

"Why are you under arrest?"

"I endangered you."

"Endangered me? You saved my life . . ."

"That isn't how Commander Sherry sees it, and he's right. I shouldn't have taken you off across the prairie to a roadhouse full of down-and-outs." He shrugged. "He called me on it, and I stand corrected." He peeled another card off the coffee-stained deck and tossed it on the cot. "You're an officer's wife."

Flushed with exasperation, Glynette folded her skirt behind her and sat on the cot beside Tom. "I may be an officer's wife, but I am first a person . . . a woman who can make decisions for herself. You did not *take* me anywhere. I chose to go. I was tired of the dull gray my life had been painted and wanted to find out if there were anything else on the palette."

Turning, she saw the magazine reader watching them wide-eyed over the top of his magazine. He'd been so interested in what he was hearing that it took him an extra moment to bring the magazine back up to his nose.

Glynette ignored him. She suddenly didn't care who heard what she had to say. "I did find something else on the palette, a bold, vibrant hue that I didn't even know existed." She stood. "No one can punish you for giving that to me."

Tom sighed and started to speak, but Glynette was already sweeping down the aisle between the cots toward the door.

Moments later Glynette stood, breathless, before the door of Captain and Dinah Sherry's quarters, midway down officers' row. She smoothed her skirts and did her best to compose her features, then pulled the gong. A graying infantry man answered the door with an affected air of grandeur. "Good evening, Mrs. McCrae," the striker said with a small bow.

She stepped into the foyer, her heart thumping so heavily and her breath so short she could hardly speak. "Good evening, Horton. I'd like to see Captain Sherry."

Before the striker could fetch his employer, Frank Allen Sherry emerged from the parlor with a strained smile. "Mrs. McCrae, what a surprise!"

Glynette's Corporal

"Excuse me for getting right to the point, Captain Sherry," Glynette began with as much politeness as she could muster, "but I just came from the hospital, and I understand you are detaining my striker. There must be some misunderstanding."

Frank glanced nervously toward the parlor, then smiled solicitously. "Why don't you come inside and sit down? Mrs. Sherry will be so happy to see you. We've all been quite worried about you."

Glynette stared at him.

"And of course we can discuss the situation involving your striker."

"I'm sorry, but I must decline," Glynette said coolly, knowing that Dinah was in the parlor, straining every nerve in an effort to overhear. "Please give my regrets to Mrs. Sherry and thank her for her concern, but I'd simply like to have this misunderstanding resolved as quickly as possible, so that my striker can return to his position, and I can return to my home."

Frank flushed, astonished by Mrs. McCrae's bold behavior. Nothing in her demeanor suggested she felt the least guilt or shame about her recent misadventure with her striker. Any other woman in her fragile position would display contrition over her foolishness, try to win sympathy, and attempt to lay to rest any suspicion that she had given herself to a common soldier. Yet, if Dinah had told it accurately, Mrs. McCrae had rejected all overtures of sympathy. Now she was addressing him alone in his foyer, in contempt of all decorum, demanding that he undo his courtly efforts to restore her damaged reputation.

Earlier he had pooh-poohed his wife's certainty that something had happened between Mrs. McCrae and Corporal Flint. He had derided her and her friends—"the pestilence in petticoats" he called them—as bored busybodies. But suddenly the notion didn't seem so silly.

Could it be?

He drank in her beauty. Deep bosom, full mouth—very ripe, very inviting. A woman packaged like that wouldn't be content to sit around in her rocker every night. Her lips were parted slightly, showing the fine white teeth between her lips. Her wide, almond-shaped eyes were sharp now, but in bed they would be smoky. Yes, such a woman could easily grow restless. He was becoming more and more convinced it was true—last night this delicious minx relieved her frustrations with a soldier.

He felt suddenly furious with himself for not realizing sooner that he could have her himself. Why would she settle for a common soldier when she could have a man of his stature. Unconsciously, he smoothed his black mustache and pulled his shoulders back.

He smiled imperially. "Mrs. McCrae, I'm quite sure that your husband would approve of the actions I have taken. That man Flint behaved recklessly and has shown himself unfit to serve you. I know this is an inconvenience, but tomorrow I will personally choose a qualified replacement and send him over to you. In the meantime—"

"My husband isn't here to approve or disapprove of any actions you take," Glynette interjected, her eyes flashing. "But you're correct when you say you are inconveniencing me. Your treatment of my striker is appalling. He has disobeyed no order. You have no grounds to hold him."

Sherry glanced again toward the parlor. "Please, Mrs. McCrae, you mustn't get upset. I can appreciate your point of view, but these actions were necessary. Corporal Flint behaved recklessly and endangered you." He bore deeply into her eyes. "I hate to think what might have happened to you out there."

Receiving only her cold stare, he cleared his throat and added, "I'll tell you what . . . for you, I will give the matter some thought. Of course, we must keep Corporal Flint under arrest for now."

She opened her mouth to object.

He held up a hand. "The other men must know that reckless actions will not go unpunished," he said hurriedly. "But, we will not decide yet what is to happen later. It's best for your striker that he remain in the hospital for tonight, anyway. Don't you agree?"

Reluctantly she nodded.

"Suppose I pop by your quarters tomorrow morning to discuss the matter further. I'm sure we can find a compromise agreeable to us both." He gazed at her warmly. "Let's sleep on it."

An absolutely irrational part of Glynette wanted to scream and kick until this pompous fool had released Tom, but she knew that such an outburst would not help her cause. Tom was better off in the hospital for now, and if the captain was willing to discuss a compromise tomorrow, it was in her best interest to show herself to be agreeable.

"That sounds reasonable enough," she said coolly, dropping her hand to the doorknob. "I expect to be home all morning, so come by when you like."

"I'll come by first thing," he said, beaming. "Let me get my hat, and I'll walk you to your door."

She pulled the door open. "That won't be necessary, Captain. I'll see you tomorrow."

Before he could object, she had hurried down the porch steps and disappeared down the boardwalk. He stepped onto the veranda and stood for a moment in the cool evening air, listening to the soft click of her steps on the boardwalk fade into silence. Across the parade, he could hear soldiers on the porch of the infantry barracks, passing the time. A couple of drunken men exploded into laughter. A staggering man pushed his drunken companion toward the barracks in a wheelbarrow provided by the post trader for that purpose.

They drank to dispel the interminable boredom of the place, Sherry thought. How well he understood. He himself had been moldering at this post for nearly three years, with little to do but drink and play cards. The months had progressed one into the other in a kind of slow funeral march. Until now. Now it was spring, Glynette McCrae was here alone, and his surroundings suddenly seemed quite exotic. The blood pulsed in his head. For the first time in many months, Frank Allen Sherry felt he had something to anticipate.

The next morning, after a breakfast eye-opener of whiskey, water, bitters, and a half teaspoon of sugar, Captain Sherry took especial care with his toilet, slipping into a new dress shirt and securing the cuffs with his best amethyst buttons. He applied oil to his freshly washed hair and combed the wavy black locks away from his broad, handsome forehead. Though he wanted to apply a bit of cologne, he didn't dare, for he might arouse Dinah's sharp suspicions. He hoped she would not notice the amethysts beneath the sleeves of his best dress coat.

After trimming and carefully combing his long, neat mustache, he at last stood straight and stared into his own eyes in the mirror. He gave himself a sultry smile and a deeply passionate gaze and imagined the effect they would have on Glynette McCrae. He had thought of little else the previous evening as he sipped cognac before the fire, ignoring, as best he could without incurring her wrath, Dinah's incessant prattling.

He had ruminated on Glynette McCrae's beauty and his own handsomeness until he had convinced himself that he was meant to have her. A raven-haired beauty such as her must be a hotbed of passion, and that heat was most certainly wasted on the pale, anemic Anniston McCrae. He believed he could almost smell her frustrated desire and knew that a swarthy man like himself, a man to match her own dark radiance, was what she craved.

Oh, what an idiot he had been to waste so much precious time! She had been here for weeks, and though he had admired her as every man in garrison had admired her, he had imagined her bound by conventional piety to her wedding vows. But what did it matter? The thing would have been tricky to achieve under Anniston's nose, but now that he was gone, she was not only deliciously accessible, but, oh, how lonely she—

"Frank!" Dinah poked her head into the bedroom. "What are you doing? I've called you three times."

Frank jumped and turned to his wife. "Good Lord, Dinah, must you shriek like that? What in heaven's name is it?"

"Are you all right?" she drawled in her Kentucky accent.

"I'm quite all right, Dinah. What is it?"

"What should I order for dinner?"

Frank was normally quite particular about his dinner and liked to decide the menu himself in the morning, so he could anticipate the repast all day. But this morning he had given the matter no thought. He leaned over and pecked his wife on the forehead.

"Why don't you decide? It'll be a surprise for me."

Dinah eyed him suspiciously, but said nothing. She knew he was going to Mrs. McCrae's quarters, and it had not escaped her notice that he was taking unusual care with his toilet. However, with no concrete grounds for accusation, she could say nothing. If she expressed her suspicions, he would only make her out to be a jealous harridan.

"What are you going to do about Mrs. McCrae's striker?"

"I haven't decided."

Dinah recognized the tone. He would say no more than that. She turned and descended the stairs.

Frank Allen reached for his watch and clicked open the cover of the case. Seven o'clock. He would call at 7:30—early enough that he and the delectable Mrs. McCrae would have the remainder of the morning uninterrupted before the ladies started their rounds.

Glynette McCrae sat on a straightback chair in her parlor at 7:30 watching Captain Frank Allen Sherry help himself to a drink from her liquor cabinet. She was not particularly surprised at his request for a drink so early in the morning, for many of the officers drank in what they considered a manly fashion.

She was surprised, however, that he had called so early. She had only just finished dressing and was looking forward to a quiet cup of tea in the parlor when she'd heard the knock at the door. But she was not sorry he was there, for she was anxious to have Tom cleared of all charges, and she must appeal to this man to do that.

When Captain Sherry encouraged her to join him in a drink, she graciously declined. She offered him a cup of tea, he declined. He tried again. Holding up a bottle, he said, "Come, after what you've been through, a glass of Anniston's old Madeira would do you good."

"Really, it's a little early for me. Thank you, Captain," she insisted.

He looked crestfallen. She didn't notice. She studied him as one would a fallen log over a path or some other obstacle, considering the most judicious way to approach it. She must persuade the man to drop all charges against Tom and forget any delusion he might have that he had the authority to fire her striker. Before she could decide on her opening words, the captain spoke.

"I have released your striker, Mrs. McCrae, so whatever pretty speech you are forming in your mind to persuade me to do so is wasted."

She was taken aback. "But . . . last night you seemed so determined . . ."

He sipped his whiskey and smiled down on her magnanimously. "I've had all night to think on it, dear lady, and frankly what I thought was that I could not bear to disappoint you. I could not bear the thought of even a shred of unhappiness in your heart, so the first thing I did this morning was to go to the hospital myself to dismiss the guard and tell the surgeon to release your striker as soon as he is fit."

Frank smiled broadly, anticipating her gratitude.

Sensing his expectation, Glynette looked appropriately delighted. "I'm most grateful, Captain Sherry. Can he return to work?"

"That we must discuss," he said with an air of importance, leaning forward and puffing his whiskey breath over her.

Glynette felt a faint shiver of apprehension.

"Do you really want a soldier like that as your striker? After all, he endangered your life, Mrs. McCrae. I can hardly bear to think of it." He looked at her gravely and staggered slightly. He repeated the movement so it seemed intentional.

She looked grave in return. "I do, Captain."

He sipped his drink and smiled benevolently. "There's an infantryman in my company who could replace Flint. He's an older man, a man of honor and decorum and exemplary judgment. I think he would serve you well."

Glynette dropped her gaze to the floor and considered her response. She must find the right words to sway this inebriated, self-important boor, who would make his decision according to his own whim. Her instincts told her she must use her feminine influence to achieve her purpose, for Frank Allen Sherry was a man who was most overly conscious of himself as a man. She knew the type, not at all unlike her own husband—West Point men who assume their Eastern pedigree and brass buttons make them irresistible to women, and who bristle visibly when proven otherwise.

She raised her eyes to him. "Captain," she began, smiling sweetly, "I do so appreciate your concern. With Anniston gone, it's good to know you're looking out for me."

Frank lifted his chin and a look of pleasure stole over his face. Glynette set down her teacup, stood, and paced in front of the fireplace, groping for words. He watched her, enthralled. She shimmered in fresh lavender drapes. Her skirts rustled slightly as she moved. Her brow furrowed slightly in thought. He almost rushed forward to seize her, but at the last moment turned and poured himself another drink.

"It's just that my life has been disrupted so much," she continued. "I've scarcely settled into a routine at Fort Reynolds, and here I am suddenly without my husband or my servant. While I'm sure your man is worthy, I would have to begin again with him. I have established a rapport with my current striker. He is familiar with my needs . . . with what I need . . . to have done around the house."

A quick blush stole up her throat, throwing her into a fit of consternation. Frank Allen was delighted with her pose of distress. He rushed to her side and took her hand.

"Dear Mrs. McCrae, think no more of it. You shall have your striker back."

Glynette resisted the impulse to shrink back. "Thank you, Captain Sherry," she said sincerely, looking into his red-rimmed eyes.

Glynette's Corporal

Frank Allen continued to hold her hand. He bore into her eyes with his. "Mrs. McCrae, you are an absolute tearing beauty."

She kept her gaze steady, but a chill of dismay rushed over her. He moved toward her as if to kiss her. She took a step back and turned quickly aside.

"I am quite relieved to have all this resolved, Captain. I can't thank you enough," she said lightly, hoping to invite his departure. Instead, he stepped forward, closing the space between them again.

"It must be difficult for such an extraordinarily beautiful woman and exquisite young society lady as you to be buried in the frontier during the best years of her life."

Glynette attempted to relieve the tension with a laugh. "I don't see myself as much of a society lady. Anniston says I am much too awkward to do well socially."

He shaped his mouth into a laugh, but his eyes showed less mirth than desire. "I think that is to your credit. You have too much energy and intelligence to be a perfect lady."

Though he said it as a compliment, the comment was impertinent, and she did not thank him for it. Wanting him only to leave, she behaved as if she had heard nothing.

He took her hand again. "You aren't the kind of woman who can spend her days happily at quilting bees. You impress me as a woman who needs a great deal of . . . stimulation, else she grows bored."

"I'm sorry if I make that impression on you. I don't think it's a nice impression to make," she said coldly.

"You make a stunning impression," he said meaningfully. He moved toward her again, and this time, before she could turn away, he caught her by the waist and held her to him.

"Captain, please," Glynette protested, smelling the

liquor on his breath and wondering how much he'd had before he'd arrived.

"Call me Frank."

"Let me go."

"You know that isn't really what you want," Sherry said, snaking his right arm up her back, pressing his face to hers.

Trying to wriggle out of the man's stubborn grip, Glynette said, "Let me go, or I'll scream!"

He lowered his lips to hers. Glynette screamed and pulled away, stumbling over his foot. He tried to grab her but in doing so lost his own balance, and the two of them fell over a tea table. Glynette tried to get up, but the drunken captain lay atop her, his heavy, curling mustache enveloping her face, his wet lips still searching for hers.

Her back ached from the fall, and he had one of her legs pinned at an awkward angle. She moaned and said hoarsely, "Please let me up."

"Only if you promise to be nice," he said playfully.

She struggled, trying to kick and push him off of her. It did nothing but arouse the man more. He continued to chuckle and kiss her. His weight pressed the breath from her, and her efforts to scream came out as feeble groans. Exhausted from the effort, she had closed her eyes, trying to think what to do. Only she was unable to do anything except gasp in pain while Sherry ran kisses and nibbles up and down her neck.

Suddenly she felt the weight upon her lighten. She opened her eyes to see Captain Sherry's face and chest move away from her as though he had been lifted by invisible ceiling ropes. His expression went from one of drunken lust to indignant surprise.

"Hey . . . wha—" Then he wheeled on wobbly feet and went flying across the davenport.

Tom Flint appeared over Glynette, his face flushed

with fury. He had started to bend down to help her up when Sherry flew at him from the davenport. Tom pivoted to one side, grabbing the captain by his collar and giving him one short but resolute smack to the face. The man backed up, eyes wide, and grabbed his nose. The backs of his legs hit a chair and he sat down unceremoniously, grabbing his nose and rocking back against the wall.

"Mrs. McCrae," Tom said, turning to her again, and kneeling. "Are you all right?"

Glynette looked around at the upturned tea table, the captain sitting in the armchair, his head thrown back, holding his nose. "I think so," she said. She swallowed and caught her breath, brushing the hair from her face.

"Is anything broken?" he asked her.

She shook her head. Her pulse throbbed in her temples. "No . . . I don't think so." She saw that he was wincing with pain. "Tom, your side . . ."

"I'm all right."

She let him lift her to her feet. She avoided looking toward the wanton Sherry puffing in the chair just feet away, his eyes bright with rage. He held to his nose a white handkerchief, now stained a deep red.

"Where did you come from?" she asked.

"I was just coming in the back door to pick up my things, and I heard a crash."

Sherry held the handkerchief away from his nose and got heavily to his feet. "Do you realize that you just *struck* an officer?" he raged.

Tom turned to the captain. "If you ever touch Mrs. McCrae again, I'll do more than break your nose."

Sherry gave a caustic laugh, his shoulders bobbing. "Why, you insubordinate cur! I will have you flogged to within an inch of your life!" He turned toward the door.

"I'm sure you will, sir," Tom allowed, his voice matter-of-fact. "But my promise is still good. If you try anything like this again, I'll kill you."

"I'm calling the corporal of the guard!" Sherry bellowed, stomping into the hallway.

Glynette stepped into his path before he reached the door. "If you do, Captain, I'll have you arrested as well ... for assault!" Glynette's eyes were bright with challenge. The appearance of the indomitable Tom Flint had filled her with a sand, as they put it out here, like she had never known.

"What are you talking about?" Sherry grunted. His thoughts were foggy, and he couldn't quite follow the sequence of events. One moment he had Mrs. McCrae in a pleasurable embrace; now she was shouting at him, but he couldn't remember exactly why. His nose throbbed miserably.

"Call the guard, Captain, and you'll find out," Glynette said. "I'll have you court-martialed and thrown out of the Army."

Sherry's eyes were two molten steel marbles on both sides of the big hand holding the handkerchief to his nose. He gestured to Tom, standing just inside the parlor looking somewhat amused. "That soldier struck me."

"That soldier is a gentleman, which is more than I can say for you," Glynette said calmly. "Yesterday he saved my life, and if anything happens to him because he came to my rescue today, as well, I'll see that you leave the Army with your reputation in tatters. And if Anniston finds out what you've done, you might leave with more than that in tatters."

Sherry stared at her, the epitome of mute hate, considering her threat. He had done nothing. He had been brutally attacked without provocation. It would be her word—and that of a common soldier—against his. He blinked to bring her into focus. Oh, what a sultry beauty she had seemed, but she was a hard, cold shrew like all the rest. She would pay; both of them would pay. He pushed her roughly aside and grasped the door handle.

As he pulled open the door and opened his mouth to shout the alarm, a vague thought penetrated the fog in Frank's mind. He was drunk. He had been arrested before for drunkenness, for yelling epithets at the sentinels and disturbing the peace. If the guard came now, everyone would know he was drunk again. He turned to look at Glynette. This black-haired harlot would have the petticoat squad over here telling them lies. He would have to explain to Dinah. There would be a scandal. His reputation . . . he swallowed and blinked, crestfallen.

He closed the door and considered the situation.

"Do we have an understanding, Captain?" Glynette asked softly.

He looked at her askance. "You won't mention this incident to Anniston?"

"I'll say as much about it as you do."

Sherry stared at her some more, blinking the two of her into one. At length he slid his eyes to Flint, and snarled without saying anything. The door opened and slammed closed, and he was gone.

Glynette expelled a sigh of relief. "What did you mean about picking up your things?"

Tom stooped to set a tea table up right. "I figured it would be better if I went back to barracks. After what happened, it won't look good if—"

She cut him off. "I don't care how it looks. I don't want you to leave."

"People are gonna talk this thing to death."

"Let them. They're going to talk anyway. If you leave the house, they'll only find something significant in that."

He sighed and smoothed a hand over his chestnut hair, wondering what to do. He was in love with a woman who belonged to another man. That her husband was a worthless lout who didn't deserve a woman like her unfortunately didn't matter. He needed time to think. "Right now I've got to get back to the hospital," he said. "The surgeon just let me out to get my things."

He turned and disappeared down the hall. After the door slammed, Glynette pushed aside the curtains and stood staring out the window at his diminishing form. She knew he would not be back.

Chapter Seven

On a warm morning in mid-June, Maggie Lewis clutched the rim of the kitchen sink, her head spinning and her legs so weak she could barely stand. She dropped to her knees then sat on the kitchen floor.

Clearly it was going to be one of her bad days, and she now regretted sending Joe, her Chinese servant, into Harding with the morning carriage. She had ordered him to buy cloth for new summer dresses for the girls and herself, cloth she could have easily bought at the post trader's. But poor Joe rarely got out of the house, and she sometimes sent him to Harding as much for his sake as to run her errands. It was the only time he ever saw another Asian face. What a life he had, she thought as she closed her eyes and leaned against a scarred leg of the work table—a foreigner in a foreign land, with his strange silk coats and waist-length queue, scraping out his living as a servant on a remote army post.

At length she rose again, holding on to the table edge for support. Wisps of steam were just beginning to curl up from the tea kettle on the cook stove. When her legs felt steady beneath her, she reached to the cupboard for the tin of English breakfast tea, filled a strainer with the loose leaves, and returned the container to the cupboard.

She leaned against the table again, waiting for the water to boil. The lamp on the mantel above the stove still burned where Joe had placed it while he prepared breakfast. She reached up. Her grip was weak as she clutched the base of the lamp and, in one collapsing motion, her arm and the lamp came down onto the stove.

The lamp shattered against the hot surface, turning the oil to flame. Streams of flaming oil swam across the smooth iron like something alive, rushing to the edge and leaping onto Maggie's skirts so quickly she hardly knew what had happened. Her skirts flared as the burning oil caught them, and Maggie fell back against the table staring in horror. She struck at the flames with her hands, but the fire spread easily up the folds of the cloth.

For a helpless moment, she stared at her burning skirts, then turned and ran up the long hallway. Flames trailing behind her, she ran past the parlor where Ned played on his blanket, to the front door. As she passed him she screamed, "Oh, God, Neddie!" By the time she reached the door and her hand grasped the knob, her hair was aflame and what emerged from the house and stumbled across the porch looked to the soldier who first saw it like a living torch.

They did not bury Maggie until a courier had been sent for Jim. The body was wrapped in a blanket and placed in a corner of the icehouse by the river. A wake was held in the Lewis' quarters for three days. When neither the courier nor Jim had returned by the third day, Captain Sherry thought it fit to plan the funeral for the fourth. There had already been complaints about having the body in the icehouse.

All that morning Glynette had listened to the pounding

of hammers as the coffin was built, and in the afternoon, she and Agnes Johnson had fashioned a lining for it from the white silk of Maggie's wedding dress.

Glynette had borne Maggie's death with stoicism, her features an impenetrable mask. The morning of the accident, she had quietly moved into Maggie's house to care for the children until their father's return. Her heart had turned to lead the first time Ned looked around in confusion and called, "Mama?" Though she had comforted the little girls as they lay in bed holding each other and crying inconsolably, she had kept her own grief buried, knowing that if it surfaced, she would be of no use to the children.

The next morning a solemn gathering formed around a freshly dug grave among the small crosses in the cemetery north of the post. To one side of the grave, officers in full dress uniform leaned on their sabres, caps in hand, heads bowed reverently. On the other side the women dressed uniformly in black held each other and wept audibly into their handkerchiefs. Maggie's children huddled against Glynette, and she held Ned in her arms.

The post had no chaplain, so after the body was lowered into the grave, Lieutenant Grimsley, officer of the day, read from the Bible and prayed. "We give thanks," he concluded, "for the good example of all Thy servants who, having finished their course in faith, do now rest from their labors."

Because Maggie was not a soldier, no cannon was fired, but after the first shovelful of dirt was thrown on the casket and Lieutenant Grimsley had said, "Earth to earth, dust to dust," a bugler played taps. And when the melancholy strains had faded on the ceaseless prairie wind, life for most of the fort resumed its normal course.

After Jim Lewis returned, Glynette offered to care for the children until other arrangements had been made. Jim gratefully accepted the offer, as he was bewildered and grieving and could not care for his three children.

Glynette was grateful for the company, even that of three heartbroken children grieving for their mother. She was glad to be there to comfort them. Tom had returned to barracks, and with no one at home but Kola to break the silence, her loneliness and grief for Maggie would have been unbearable without them.

In late June, Glynette heard hooves thunder across the hard-packed parade and looked out the parlor window in time to see a courier rein up and mount the steps to headquarters. The soldier's horse was dark with sweat, its breath coming in harsh gasping wheezes.

Glynette left Ned napping on his blanket, picked up Kola, and stepped onto the porch. Other women began to emerge from their quarters down officers' row, some gathering on the parade to confer in urgent whispers. It was the second time a courier had ridden in with news from the battalion. The first time the news had been only of further depredations by the Indians. Though the troops had been pursuing the renegades northwest, the wily Indians had dispersed and disappeared, fragmenting the troops and eluding them, until the trails had completely vanished and the battalion was left searching for clues. In the meantime, renegades had struck a ranchhouse, brutally torturing and killing the inhabitants.

The women sensed this time was different. The courier had ridden in hell for leather, refusing to speak to anyone, his face aghast. Glynette held Kola to her chest, her eyes glued to the door of headquarters. She heard the sound of a door behind her and turned to see Lucy and Dolly. Lucy's face was uncharacteristically sallow.

"The way that man flew in here, something's happened," she said knowingly.

When the door to headquarters opened and the courier

Glynette's Corporal 149

emerged, the women descended their porch steps. The laundresses had drifted down from suds row, and they, too, walked stiffly toward the courier, their features paralyzed in attitudes of dread. The soldier hurriedly mounted his lathered horse, trying to ignore pleas from the women for the contents of the dispatch. He said nothing, only shook his head sympathetically and turned his horse toward the stables. Several of the women stood in front of the horse. A laundress clutched the man's leg and wailed, "Ruger, please, tell us."

"What's happened? Please tell us," the rest of the women joined the chorus, until the courier cast a nervous glance toward headquarters and said hurriedly, "There's been a battle. The renegades are finished. I can't say any more."

He clucked his horse urgently and broke through the crowd of women as they assimilated this cryptic message. It told them nothing. The only information that mattered to each woman was the answer to the question, "Is my husband alive?"

Glynette checked on Ned and left Kola inside, then she and Lucy joined the other women gathered at headquarters. In a few minutes the door to headquarters opened again and Captain Sherry emerged, his face blanched but otherwise revealing nothing. The women moved in closer to hear what he would say.

"The renegades were found taking refuge with a band camped near the Canadian border," he announced. "A battle was fought. All the renegades and members of that band have been killed or captured . . . the region is safe again for the time being." He paused and studied their faces. "The price for peace was the lives of twelve soldiers . . ."

The women collectively drew in their breaths. Their minds raced. Only twelve dead out of more than one hundred and fifty men. The odds were good for any of them . . . but odds didn't matter if one of the twelve was your husband.

"Tell us the names!" one of the laundresses shouted. Several others echoed her. The officers' wives remained silent, but they stared at Captain Sherry with dark, imploring eyes, and several nodded mute encouragement to the captain.

"I have the names of the dead." He held a sheet of paper up. "It might be easier for you if I come to your quarters . . ."

This time the officers' wives joined the wailing chorus. "Tell us now!" They all looked around at each other to see if anyone objected, but the laundresses and the ladies all wore the same desperate look that said they were about to storm the porch and snatch away the paper that held their fate.

Sherry held up a hand. "I'll read the names. I'll read them in the order they are listed. They do not appear to be in any particular order . . ."

He swallowed. The first two were unmarried soldiers, but he'd noticed that the third name on the list was Sergeant Ted Falk, Second Cavalry, Company B—a fat-bellied, good-natured father of three. They called him Teddy. Captain Sherry's eyes instinctively picked out Teddy's wife in the group before him. The hard-faced woman clung to another laundress, her chin stoically lifted, her eyes gleaming with dread. He tore his eyes away from her face. *Oh God, just read the names.*

He cleared his throat. "Private Luther Weide, Fourth Infantry, Company H . . . Private Henry Russell, Second Cavalry, Company B . . ."

After each name one or more of the laundresses moaned or wept, those who did laundry for the fallen man or counted him as a friend.

"... First Sergeant Ted Falk, Second Cavalry, Company B ..."

As Glynette listened to the names called above the sound of the wailing laundresses, she grew more and more shaky. In spite of everything that had happened between them, she dreaded hearing Anniston's name read. She dreaded hearing the name of anyone she knew.

Captain Sherry had meant to read the list in a steady rhythm without pause, but when he named Ted Falk, several screams arose, and the women converged upon Ted Falk's widow. He lifted his eyes, missing a beat, but quickly recovered and read the next name.

"Private Pierre Ropier, Second Cavalry, Company E ..."

Glynette's stomach flipped. Tom's company. She offered up a silent prayer of thanks that Tom had not been with Company E and wondered if Pierre Ropier had been Tom's friend.

The end of the list was near. The thought had just begun to form in Glynette's mind: No one she knew had died. Then the syllables of the next name arrested her heart in mid-beat and the June sun dimmed around her.

"First Lieutenant Gregor Britzman, Second Cavalry, Company E."

What happened after that Glynette could never remember. A cry escaped her throat, her hands covered her face, and immediately something in her closed up. She didn't think, didn't feel, and as she lifted her head, everything around her moved slowly as though existing out of human time. She turned to Lucy and saw that Lucy appeared to be turned to stone. After an eternity Lucy took a single step forward, her eyes burning brightly.

Glynette moved toward her as if moving through water. Lucy's face twisted and grew white, her mouth opened, and she wailed with a breath that stretched far on the wind the sound of her husband's name. Just as her knees buckled, Glynette reached her, but Glynette could not catch the massive woman, and the two of them toppled to the ground and lay in a heap, blinded by the prairie sun, until the others stooped over them and blocked out the light.

Three days later the battalion returned, little resembling the group that had left several weeks before. The men were sunburned, dusty, and haggard, many sporting blood-stained bandages. Their uniforms were dirty, tattered, and sloppily patched. Many of them had grown beards, so that their wives and friends didn't recognize them.

The horses, too, looked beleaguered, and several had heavy bundles tied across their backs, the bodies of fallen troopers wrapped in their blankets. Eight Indians, tied together in a line, wrists bound, followed behind two of the wagons. In the wagons lay the critically injured and more bodies of the dead, including that of Lieutenant Gregor Britzman, the only officer who died.

The rest of the afternoon, as they stabled their horses, unpacked their gear, and filed into the washrooms, the weary troopers listened to the sounds of hammers pounding from the quartermaster's yards. The men in garrison had been detailed to build coffins and dig graves for their fallen comrades. The twelve soldiers would have to be buried quickly. Their bodies had already lain out too long in the warm June sun, but Major Johnson, who had caught an arrow in the shoulder and was ailing himself, hadn't the heart to bury the soldiers on the open prairie when they might instead lie close to the people who loved them.

Anniston alone did not look battle-weary. He sat straight in his saddle, still wearing his undaunted smile.

Glynette's Corporal

His uniform, though sporting a small tear at the knee, was scrupulously neat given the circumstances, and, except for his carefully trimmed trooper's mustache, he remained clean shaven. Later he would brag to Glynette that he had proven himself a skilled Indian fighter in his first frontier battle. His fame would grow in Washington as a result of his exploits.

The Sioux, well-armed with repeating rifles, had fought tenaciously, but Anniston had led his company to the forefront, seizing the momentum from the start. He didn't tell his wife that the Army troops had descended upon the camp as the Indians slept, or that they had slaughtered women and children as indiscriminately as the Sioux had slaughtered the whites.

At the funeral the next morning, the entire garrison and a smattering of civilians stood around twelve freshly dug graves. While scriptures were read, a salute fired, and taps played, Glynette felt numb. In less than a month she had lost two people dear to her, two people who had made life at Fort Reynolds bearable.

As the last notes of taps faded, the mourners made shuffling movements to disperse. Suddenly the band, drums covered in black crepe, struck up a lively tune and, upon orders, the troops began a double-time march back to the fort.

Glynette was shocked at the festive music. Agnes Johnson, seeing her expression, said, "Dear girl, the morale of the soldiers must be bolstered. They cannot stop to mourn."

"I think a bit of mourning would be better," Glynette said, staring with dismay after the raucous band and marching soldiers.

The old Army wife put an arm around the younger one and gave her a sympathetic squeeze. "We must try to keep the Army spirit, dear," she said, with only a trace of irony, "and know that our friend Gregor will have a joyous waking at the great reveille."

On the Fourth of July, the garrison awoke to the sound of the band playing patriotic melodies at reveille. It was a day away from the monotony of fatigue duties for the men, and for everyone a day of feasting, festivities, and games from sunrise until well into the night.

The day dawned still and clear. It was already warm, with a haze of sun-powdered dust hanging over the parade ground. After guard mount, the officers and troops assembled around the flag pole and listened while the band played "The Star Spangled Banner." Major Johnson read the Declaration of Independence and the artillery fired a salute of thirty-eight guns, one for each state.

Then a picnic was held in the clearing west of the fort along the river. Several pigs roasted on spits. A long table was laden with canned delicacies, fresh bread, and cakes. The post trader had generously provided two wagons filled with bottles of champagne and brandy, and more kegs of beer than the whole garrison of thirsty revelers could finish in a day.

Blankets and picnic cloths lined the river as everyone sought a patch of shade. Groups of laundresses sat with their children. Soldiers lounged in the sun and lazily swilled the post trader's beer. Here and there a soldier flirted with his sweetheart from town. Separate from all of these were the groups of officers and their families.

That afternoon, after many of the revelers had fallen asleep on their blankets, and the only activity was a sleepy baseball game, Anniston suggested to Glynette that they take a walk along the river. Though several other couples formed their party, Anniston did not invite them.

"Let's take a quiet little stroll, just ourselves," he said.

Glynette eyed him suspiciously, then reluctantly took

the arm her husband offered. Since his return, he had remained solicitous toward her in the presence of others, playing his habitual role of officer and gentleman. In private, however, his verbal abuse had become intolerable.

As soon as he heard about Glynette and Tom's misadventure and caught wind of the rumors, he'd immediately begun proceedings to have Tom court-martialed. Then bizarrely, he had ordered Tom to resume his duties as striker. When she'd asked him why, he had said menacingly, "Why, so you and your lover can be together."

She couldn't fathom what evil motivated him. Perhaps he hoped to catch them together. Perhaps he was simply trying to humiliate her. Whatever his motives, he had created a tension in the house that was nearly palpable. Tom tolerated the degrading position he'd been ordered to assume, but he rarely spoke. She and Tom avoided each other and did not dare occupy the same room alone. Only once Tom had stopped her in the hallway, put his strong hand gently to her face, and whispered, "You have to get out of here. Go back to Washington."

She felt she was living in a nightmare, but she couldn't leave. Tomorrow Tom would be arrested and thrown in jail. Only at the major's request had Anniston agreed to wait until after the Independence Day festivities. She was afraid of what would happen to Tom if she left. Moreover, she did not know where she would go. She no longer had a life in Washington. With the deaths of her only friends at the fort, and being cut off from Tom, she felt completely unmoored.

The desire to help Tom was all that kept her going. Though Anniston would try to stop her, she would fight the court-martial tooth and nail. She no longer cared what anyone thought. Once she knew Tom was safe, she would return to Washington and begin divorce proceedings. The thought of divorce, once inconceivable, now seemed like a mere formality. Her marriage was a sham.

Anniston led her along a narrow path forged by game, the grass rustling about them, brushed with cloud shadows. Birds twittered in the trees. He said nothing as they walked, but she sensed something was coming.

She glanced at him from the corner of her eye, a heavy weight in her chest. It seemed amazing that only a few weeks earlier, she was still trying desperately to find a way to win his love and save their marriage. Now she felt nothing for him but a longing to get away.

It was obvious he cared nothing for her either. He tried to cow her at every turn with threats and insults. He had humiliated her by keeping a concubine that everyone on the fort knew about but had condemned her for mere rumors. Ironically, though he had turned her life into a living hell, his greatest fear seemed to be that she would divorce him and thereby ruin his name and his career. Only a few days ago he had told her that if she tried to divorce him, he would destroy her. His threat had left her nonplussed. What did he imagine that he could do to her that would be worse than living with his hate, his constant assault of threats and insults?

As Anniston continued walking and saying nothing, Glynette noticed the consternation in his expression. Sensing her gaze upon him, he jerked his head up and looked at her, wild-eyed. She suddenly felt frightened.

"Anniston, what's wrong?" she gasped, recoiling from him.

Anniston's eyes shrank and became cold. "Nothing's wrong, Glynette," he said ominously. "Nothing that won't soon be righted."

From the corner of her eye Glynette saw something move through the trees. Something like a shadow.

She stopped and studied the place where the shadow had been. "I think something's out there."

He turned and followed her gaze. "I didn't see anything."

A whoop sounded in the trees off to their left, and the sound of pounding hooves thundered through the air. Glynette jerked her eyes around and saw five brilliantly painted, wild-eyed Indians bounding toward her and Anniston—whooping and screaming, hair blowing behind them, like something out of a nightmare. Glynette froze. She filled her lungs with air, but instead of a scream, only a clipped groan came from her throat.

"Indians!" Anniston cried, releasing her arm. He hesitated, then reached for his sidearm and dropped to a knee. He squeezed off two rounds before one of the Indians approached at a gallop, clubbed him in the head with a rifle stock, and lunged for Glynette.

Glynette screamed as the hot, sweaty arm grabbed her arm and yanked her off her feet, pulling her onto his horse. An arrow of pain shot through her arm as though it had been yanked from its socket, then the wind was forced from her lungs as the man threw her over his horse, reined the horse around, and started away with an ear-rattling scream.

For a moment, she lost consciousness, but the persistent, painful jarring of her belly and chest against the horse's spine quickly returned her to her senses. She couldn't breath. With each galloping lunge, the air was slammed out of her lungs as though by an angry fist, and she could almost feel her ribs cracking. Faintly, she heard men's voices and then, gradually, the intermittent cracking of guns. She lifted her head and tried to push herself off the galloping mount, but the Indian had an iron-like fist wrapped around the base of her neck, holding her fast. The sweat of the horse filled her nostrils, the taste of its mane was in her mouth.

She had ridden that way, in excruciating pain, for what seemed like hours but could only have been a few minutes when she became aware again of guns cracking behind her. Suddenly, the Indian who held her gave a wild cry, and the hand on her neck loosened and fell away. The rider's foot smacked her hard in the hip, and to her right she saw blood on his face as he fell backward, gave another cry, and disappeared in the dust kicked up by the horse.

Realizing that she was now alone on the horse, Glynette clutched its mane, trying to hold on, but without the man's hand on her back she could feel herself slipping. If only she could swing her right foot up over the horse's back and get herself into riding position, she might get the beast stopped. She attempted the maneuver, but she hadn't the strength and her skirts made it impossible to lift her leg. She realized she could not hold on and would have to drop to the ground.

Oh God, she would be trampled, she thought. Dangling as she was, she could not push away from the horse, but would simply have to drop in a heap. Just as she was about to release her tenuous hold, she heard the hooves and jangling rein chains of another approaching horse.

"Don't let go . . . hold on!" a familiar voice yelled.

But it was too late—she couldn't hold on. In the same moment she released the mane and began slipping to the ground, the horse suddenly slowed, turning, as someone grabbed its Indian bridle and coaxed it to a halt. Glynette slid down the horse's side, crumpling in a heap to the ground, gasping for breath, her entire torso burning from the pounding and chafing she'd received.

She flinched and covered her head as she heard the horse's hoofbeats start again, but they faded in the distance as the horse galloped after the others. An arm wrapped around her, lifting her, and she fell, coughing and gagging against a big, blue-covered chest that blocked the light from her eyes. Barely conscious, she looked up. Staring down at her from under the brim of his forage cap were the troubled green eyes of Tom Flint.

Anniston McCrae was furious, more furious than he'd ever been in his life, and he was having a hard time not showing it to Glynette, who led him out of the infirmary and closed the door behind them. He was wearing a thick bandage around his head, where the redskin had clubbed him hard enough to raise a lump on his head and give him a mild concussion.

"We'd better get you into bed, as the doctor ordered," Glynette said, taking her unsteady husband's arm. She was not in particularly good shape herself, though she knew she was fortunate that her injuries had amounted only to some very black bruises across her ribs and a bit of pain if she drew a deep breath.

Anniston, however, had a lump that covered half his head. It seemed a miracle that he had suffered only a mild concussion. He had refused to stay in the hospital, and the surgeon had reluctantly released him, after giving detailed instructions to Glynette as to Anniston's care and making her promise she would keep a close eye on him. Now, as they stood on the boardwalk in front of their quarters, Anniston stopped, dug in his heels, and resisted her insistent tug.

"No," he said to Glynette, worrying the small bottle of laudanum in his pocket, which the surgeon had supplied to get him through the night. "I have to talk to Captain Sherry first. I want to fill him in on what happened out there."

"Anniston, you heard what the surgeon said." Glynette felt like turning on her heel and leaving him to do as he wished, but she had promised the surgeon she would watch over him.

Anniston scowled, scarcely able to disguise the revulsion Glynette aroused in him. He could not look at her without imagining her in the arms of that common soldier. What she saw in that sub-human being, Anniston couldn't fathom. Oh, but what a prize she was for him, he knew—an officer's wife! The other dolts in the barracks must think him quite the big shot—cuckolding Captain McCrae!

The thought of it made him grind his teeth. He would see Tom Flint hung by the neck, one way or another. If there was anything to which he could not submit, it was being cuckolded. He would be rid of both of them yet. Glynette was no longer simply a poor choice, she was out of control. He had to rid himself of her before she destroyed both his reputation and his career.

"Yes, I heard the doctor," Anniston said through gritted teeth, "but I think it's important that Sherry and I discuss what we're going to do about those filthy savages who tried to kidnap you." He smiled devilishly and touched her hair, wanting to grab it and pull, but controlling himself.

She flinched and stared at him fearfully.

"When I think of what they could be doing to you right now," Anniston continued, "if the good corporal hadn't intervened on his fast horse."

Glynette stared into the wild, mesmerizing eyes of her husband. Her nerves were still raw from what she'd just been through, but suddenly she found the visage of her husband as frightening as any savage.

"Don't worry, pet," Anniston said, drawing his face close to hers. She took a step backwards and instinctively raised her arms. "I'll see to it justice is served. Now you run along home, and I'll be there in a few minutes."

Moments later Anniston was ushered by Captain Sherry's striker into Sherry's private study upstairs. The captain was reclining on a leather-upholstered fainting couch, reading a newspaper and smoking a thick cigar. He wore only an undershirt, with crescents of sweat beneath the armpits and across the stomach, and trousers, his suspenders dangling down his sides. Both windows were open, letting in a breeze through the curtains, but the room was still hot and musty, and Anniston felt himself break out in an immediate sweat. Children could be heard playing in the backyard.

"Anniston," Sherry said as he struggled into a sitting position. "How are you doing, old fellow? How's the noggin?"

"A little worse for the wear," Anniston said crisply, put off by the captain's condition. Not only did he look hideous in the sweat-stained undershirt, he'd obviously been drinking heavily. A cut glass decanter of port sat on the floor by the couch, and a half-filled tumbler rested on an arm. A liberal smattering of ashes covered the rug all around the ashtray. Anniston wondered if the sot would make it out for retreat in a half hour.

Sherry chuckled. "I guess you should have stressed to your cohorts the difference between a tap to the head and a genuine braining, eh, McCrae?"

"It's not funny, Frank."

"No, I suppose not. I have to say, though, it was a capital idea. The Indians riding in, clubbing you on the head, and carting off your wife." He held up his newspaper. "Just like the stories you read."

"Yes, complete with the hero to save the day."

Sherry's eyes darkened. "The ubiquitous Tom Flint. Why wasn't he passed out with the rest of his beer-swilling ilk?"

"Never mind, Frank, it's time for plan B. I should have known better than to concoct a plan that involved bribing savages with booze and guns."

"What are you going to do now?"

"*We*, Frank. We're in this together. Or did you forget how my lovely wife set her Cerebus on you to smash your face when you started pawing her—"

"I wasn't pawing!"

"Come on, Frank. I know what happened. You got drunk and thought you'd show her what it's like with a *real* man." McCrae laughed derisively. "And she showed you the door."

Sherry pondered the floor, sullen. "She promised she wouldn't tell you."

Anniston chuckled darkly. "She didn't. Your charming wife did."

Sherry's face blanched. "Dinah . . . ?"

Anniston barked out a laugh, then clutched his head. "Ah, God." He fished out the bottle of laudanum and brought it to his lips.

When the pain had subsided, he sneered again at Sherry. "Do you think your little wife was stupid enough to believe your nose was broken during an accident in the stables? Dinah knew you weren't at the stables that morning, Frank. She saw you come out of my house with your bloody nose." He arched his brows. "The poor girl thought it was only right that I should know what was going on between you and my wife."

For a moment Sherry looked as though he might cry. "Dinah knows. She knew . . . and she never let on . . ."

"Never mind that now, Frank. I need you to focus. Focus on getting even with Flint and my wife."

Sherry's eyes glittered. "I'll admit I'd like to get Flint."

"Then we're of a like mind."

"But your wife, Anniston . . . I don't care to see your wife . . . dead. To me she's—"

"Yes, I know what she is to you. But she should pay for

what she did to you. The first idea didn't work. I've got a better one."

Captain Sherry wagged his head drunkenly. "*Murder*, Anniston?"

"This is war, Captain, a practical matter. Don't be maudlin."

Anniston retrieved a glass from Sherry's desk and reached for the decanter at the captain's feet. The shift of blood to his head made it throb again as though an anvil had been dropped on it. He sat down with a gasp and put a hand to it gingerly, then looked at Sherry with daggers in his eyes. "By the way, I hope you gave orders not to bring any of those incompetent fools back alive."

"Of course."

Anniston sipped the port and remained still until the throbbing in his skull subsided. Then he smacked his lips. "I've another idea for my wife . . . and Flint."

Sherry, his expression doleful, poured himself another drink and poured half of it down his throat.

"Tomorrow morning before breakfast, I want you to send guards over and arrest him."

"For what?"

"Rape and murder."

"What? How?"

Anniston sipped the port and stared at Captain Sherry. "Tonight," he said casually, "the good corporal will assault my wife while I'm sleeping off the head-clubbing I received today. Then he'll cut her lovely throat."

Chapter Eight

That night, in the dark bedroom, Glynette lay next to Anniston dreaming of Indians . . . thousands of Indians racing toward her through the trees. She stood frozen, watching them, too shocked and horrified to run, her heart pounding like a tomtom. Then one of them threw her to the ground and lay atop her, his hand over her mouth, trying to suffocate her. She struggled under the hand holding her head firmly in its grip, moaning with fright. Then she heard a familiar voice in her ear.

"It's me. Don't scream."

She opened her eyes. The room was dark, but she could make out the silhouetted figure hovering over her. Tom. His hand was still over her mouth, but she drew a breath threw her nose.

"Don't scream," he whispered again.

She nodded. When the hand came away, she lifted her head to ask what was happening—her first thought was that the house was on fire. Tom shushed her with a finger to his lips. He pressed his face to her ear and said in a barely audible whisper, "Meet me downstairs." He turned and was gone, a shadow vanishing through the open door.

Glynette's Corporal

Glynette turned to look at Anniston. He lay snoring, his back to her, the white of his bandage bright atop the pillow. She slipped out of bed, drew a wrapper about her shoulders, and crept quietly downstairs. Tom was in the kitchen, where two lanterns shunted shadows across the saddlebags lying on the kitchen table. The striker was stuffing them with dried food and coffee.

"Tom," Glynette whispered, "what are you doing?"

He turned to her and put his hands on her shoulders. "I don't have time to explain. When we're on the trail—"

"*Trail*? What are you talking about?"

He stopped, set down the knapsack and squeezed her shoulders and looked urgently into her eyes. "I love you, Glynette. Do you know that?"

The pronouncement, so unexpected and straightforward, made her skin prickle. She nodded.

"Then trust me. I'll explain when we're out of here. Right now you have to go upstairs, gather some clothes—riding and traveling clothes—and come down here and dress where he won't hear you. Take only what you must. You won't be coming back."

"Tom?"

"We have to *hurry*," he rasped, pushing her toward the door.

Quickly, numbly, she climbed the stairs to her room, and gathered her clothes quietly while Anniston snored. She removed saddlebags from a shelf, set them on the floor, and stuffed them with extra clothes. Lifting the bag to her shoulder, she crept to the door.

"Hey!"

Anniston's stern voice made her freeze in her tracks. Her heart thumped as she sucked in her breath, squeezing her eyes closed. She turned to him slowly in the darkness. She hoped he couldn't see her any better than she could see him. Her mind raced for an explanation.

She swallowed. "I . . . was just—"

"There," Anniston said, cutting her off. "That'll take care of that little problem, won't it?" He sighed, rolled over, and resumed his snoring.

Glynette quietly released her breath. Her heart still thumped and her legs were weak as she left the room, carefully drew the door closed behind her, and swept quickly down the stairs, the saddlebag over her right shoulder, her left arm cradling riding clothes and boots.

In the kitchen, Tom stood waiting for her, dressed in civilian garb—fringed buckskin tunic, blue denims, undershot boots, and a cream plainsman with a cord hanging loose beneath his chin. He wore a pistol and knife on his hip and held a rifle in his hand. His hat was pulled low on his forehead.

Glynette set the saddlebag and clothes on the table. She removed the night wrapper, and Tom turned politely away as she dressed in a pair of riding pants, chemise, cotton shirt, and riding boots. Donning her hat, she noticed Tom was watching her now, the lanterns pushing shadows this way and that over his rugged face.

She picked up her saddlebags. "I'm ready."

"Here," he said, picking up an Army-issue .45 from the table. He twirled the cylinder. The click of steel sounded loud in the stillness. "This is for you."

She smiled wryly. "I still don't know how to use it."

"Just aim it and pull the trigger."

"That's all?" She snorted, accepting the gun from him and stowing it in her bag. "After all that fuss."

They crept down the hallway to the back exit. Just as they closed the door, Glynette stopped suddenly. "What about Kola?"

Tom hesitated, then opened the door to the house again. A moment later he emerged with the prairie dog under his arm, the animal gazing around, jerking its head excitedly. "I guess it's time for him to go out into the big world."

Glynette took Kola from Tom, held him to her lips, and kissed him. She pressed back her tears, making her mind a blank. "Good-bye, my sweet," she whispered. She took the animal outside and set it down in the grass, watched as it turned to her curiously, gave its little chuckle, and waddled off, sniffing at the grass.

Tom took Glynette by the hand, and they were off, stealing behind the duplexes, heading for the grove of trees behind the stables, keeping to the shadows so they wouldn't be spotted by sentries. They pulled up short in front of the storehouses, where a lone sentry paced his post along the row. They waited until he had reached the far end of his march, then slipped past him into the dark.

"I have a horse picketed in the trees," Tom said as he led her through the waist-high brush.

They found the horse, a black figure against the stygian blackness of the trees. "Easy, boy, shh," Tom whispered, as he approached, patting the horse's neck and draping his saddlebags over the horse's rump. He slipped his rifle into the scabbard attached to the saddle, the butt of the .45 caliber Spencer snugged against the horse's right front hip.

"Here," Tom said, turning to Glynette. He took her saddlebags and draped them over his own. "I couldn't get two horses from the stable without someone gettin' suspicious, so we'll have to ride double."

Glynette waited, feeling the adrenaline course through her veins, a million questions running through her mind. This was it, she thought, with a vague sense of falling, plummeting through space. Her life was changing, and in one more minute, there would be no going back . . . she was terrified.

Tom tightened the saddle's latigo and untied the bridle

reins from a branch. When he'd climbed into the leather, the horse sidestepped and pricked its ears, the leather creaking in the still night air. Tom soothed it with his quiet baritone, then held out his hand to Glynette.

"You ready to ride?"

She looked at the gloved hand, her heart pounding, the breath careening in and out of her lungs. She took one resolute step forward and gave him her hand. "I'm ready."

With a swift tug, he lifted her gently up behind him. He clucked to the horse, and they were off at a canter, heading in the direction of Harding. When they were a mile from the fort, Tom slowed the horse to a walk. The night was so clear, the stars gleamed, and the lights of Harding glowed in the northeastern sky. Tom turned his head so he could see Glynette from the corner of his eye. He hesitated.

"Tom, tell me what's going on."

He faced up the trail. "Those Indians that attacked you yesterday . . . he hired them."

"What?"

"Captain McCrae hired those Indians to kidnap you . . . most likely to kill you."

"How do you know that?"

He turned his head to the side again. "The way those Indians came galloping into the picnic, they'd never do that on their own. I saw the captain shoot at them, he was purposely throwing his shots wide."

"*Why?*" Glynette rasped, incredulous. It was too extraordinary. People didn't . . . Anniston wouldn't . . .

"For one thing, he suspects we're having an affair."

"But murder?"

"Captain Sherry's in on it too."

"Tom, I can't believe this fantastic story you're telling me. What proof do you have?"

"Horton, Sherry's striker, is an eavesdropper and a gossip. After Sherry attacked you, I got a lot more interested in Horton's gossip. To make a long story short, Captain McCrae visited Sherry in his office last night. They concocted a plan."

"What plan?" she whispered, a chill creeping up her spine.

Tom hesitated. "To kill you and make it look like I did it. Sherry was going to go along with it to get back at both of us."

Glynette stared at Tom's back, her mind a fog of mixed emotions. She knew that Anniston despised her and would love to be rid of her. She also knew that his diabolic temper had been kept in check only by fear of a scandal. But that he would murder her . . .

"You okay?"

"What are we going to do?"

"For starters we're going to get as far away from here as we possibly can. Hold on." He kicked the horse into a ground-eating lope. Glynette turned to look behind them, half afraid she'd see Anniston riding them down.

Anniston awakened just as the back door clicked shut.

He had heard a distant stirring in his sleep, but it took awhile to swim up through the laudanum fog and open his eyes. Groggily, he turned his head toward Glynette. It was too dark to see anything more than her form beneath the sheet. Seeing her there, sleeping quietly, he stiffened at the duty he had before him, his mind growing wakeful and lucid, the laudanum folding back like the wake of a boat's prow. He lay back on his pillow, plotting each move he would make.

He would attack Glynette, allowing her to scream enough to awaken Flint, who would come to investigate. Before Flint arrived, he would slit her throat, then shoot the striker as he entered the room. The captain's story would be that he was sleeping downstairs, because he hadn't wanted to disturb his dear wife with his snoring, a side-effect produced by the laudanum. He woke during the night and heard a commotion upstairs. Going to investigate, he found the striker leaving the room with a bloody knife in his hand. The man pulled a gun on the captain, and the captain shot him.

McCrae's pulse throbbed in his injured head, a small price to pay for the jubilation he felt. How could anyone not believe the corporal had killed Glynette in a fit of passion, after all the rumors that had been flying about? He was a big brute of a man, after all.

Anniston smiled. It was a perfect plan. Corporal Flint and Glynette would get what they deserved, he himself would be free of an unworthy and burdensome wife, and his military slate would be clean.

In the semi-darkness the captain made sure his knife was still on his bedside table, under a handkerchief. Then, his heart beating insistently against his sternum, he turned to his wife. He had intended to draw the adulterous wanton to him harshly but, reaching out his hand, he grabbed nothing but the sheet and a light blanket, twisted and humped in the vague shape of a person.

She wasn't there.

Anniston stared into the darkness, thinking. He listened. She wasn't using the night vase in the closet. She wasn't upstairs at all. She must be downstairs . . . in the annex! His mouth twisted into a smile. Perfect.

He grabbed the gun and the knife, donned his slippers, and crept downstairs, taking his time on the steps so the planks wouldn't squeak. He padded noiselessly through the dark kitchen to the little annex room and stopped dead in his tracks. The door was open. It was too dark to see inside the room, but all was silent. If they were in there, they certainly wouldn't have left the door wide open.

Glynette's Corporal

He cleared his throat and softly said, "Anyone here?"

Silence. Not even the sibilance of rustling cloth.

Frowning and wary, the captain found a lantern and a box of matches. A minute later he was holding the lit lantern high in the doorway of the room off the kitchen. His pulse beat painfully in his head as he stared, befuddled, around the room—in which there was nothing but a cot, a chair, and a wardrobe. The cot was made without a wrinkle, in the military way, and the only personal effects were two pairs of uniform pants and tunics, folded carefully on the chair.

The house was silent. His wife wasn't here. The striker wasn't here. Anniston cursed, turned, and—ignoring his aching skull—ran through the kitchen, to the stairs, up the steps, and into the bedroom. He looked around the room. Most of Glynette's belongings seemed to be in their rightful place . . . all that is, except the treasured oval-framed photograph of her father which she'd kept atop her bureau.

It was gone. And that meant Glynette was gone, as well. She and the striker had left . . . together.

Anniston stood staring at the blank spot on the bureau, while a rage built up inside him, setting his very loins to boiling. The prospect of their getting away from him and making a happy life together was too much for him to bear. Not only that, but what a laughingstock he would be. Did you hear that McCrae's wife ran away with their servant? Ha ha ha!

"*No!* he shouted, slamming his fist into the wall so hard it cracked the plaster. Ignoring the pain in his head and his hand, he struggled into his clothes and planned his course of action. The striker had no doubt headed to town with his wife. The only fast way out of this country was by train. They would try to make the morning eastern-bound at 1:30. Checking his watch, Anniston saw that it was nearly midnight. He could catch them if he hurried. He'd have to go alone. He couldn't very well murder them with a detail along.

He buckled his gunbelt, picked up his rifle, donned his hat, and opened the back door. He stopped suddenly, giving a start, and dropped his gaze to the rodent Tom had given Glynette—standing on its hind legs near the door, regarding the captain curiously.

Anniston snarled. He picked up a leftover two-by-four from Tom's chicken coop construction, and Kola sensed danger. With a squeal he darted beneath the house. Anniston hurled the two-by-four after him.

"Rodent," McCrae growled, then headed toward the stables at a run.

Tom galloped as far as he dared. The horse was well-burdened, carrying two people and a pair of saddlebags. With the dark of night cloaking the terrain, a galloping horse could break its leg in a gopher hole or fox den, and they'd be stranded afoot. He brought the mount to a walk, then stopped to let the horse drink from a spring bubbling out of a hillside. The air was warm but fresh, and stars rolled over them, seemingly close enough to touch. In the far distance, coyotes yammered.

"Where are we going?" Glynette said. She still could not get her mind around what was happening. To be awakened in the night and find herself fleeing for her life with the man she loved. It was horrifying and surreal, but at the same time she felt exhilarated.

"You're going to Washington. I'm returning to the fort. With a little luck, no one will ever know I was gone."

"You're not coming with me?"

Tom chuckled softly and stroked her cheek. "Not right now. If I go AWOL, how long do you think it would take them to catch me?"

She threw her arms around his waist and buried her head against his shoulder. "But if you stay here, Anniston will have you thrown in jail tomorrow. You'll be court-martialed. If he would murder his wife in cold blood, he will try to find a way to have you hanged."

"Shh," he said, stroking her hair. "I won't be hanged. I'm sure that's what the captain wants, but the fact is, I haven't committed a hanging crime."

She looked up at him, tears glistening in the starlight. "If you stay, he'll find a way to get you."

"I can look out for myself," Tom said calmly, "and I trust the major. He knows Anniston is looking for revenge."

"What do you think will happen?"

"I'll be court-martialed and dishonorably discharged. Then I'll come find you."

He glanced down the road toward the fort. "Come on now, we have to keep moving . . ."

They made the dark-clad Harding a half-hour later, Glynette's heart drumming a panicked rhythm. She knew what the Army, at Anniston's insistence, would do to Tom if they caught him. As they rode between the two rows of false-fronted buildings to the station house, the only sounds were the barks of a town dog answering the chorus of country coyotes, and the breeze whisking under the eaves and squeaking the shingle chains over Main. Even the drunken cowboys must have all passed out for the night. One of the hideous dogs of Harding stared silently at them, then drifted down the street looking for a fight.

Lanterns had been lit on either side of the station house's front door, and several hanging lamps flickered within. Tom tied the horse to the hitchpost out front, grabbed Glynette's saddlebags, and led her through the door. There were only two other people in the place—a lanky, young man in a black drover's hat, dozing on a bench; and the station agent, moving sleepily in the shadows behind the counter.

Tom went to the counter and asked the agent for a single through-ticket to Washington. While the man did the paperwork, Tom asked him if the train was on time. "About twenty minutes late," he replied. "And please don't complain to me—I only run the station house and sell tickets, don't have nothin' to do with drivin' the train."

Tom walked over to Glynette. "The train's late. I'm going to walk down the street a ways, make sure we haven't been followed. If the train arrives before I get back, you have to promise me you'll get on it."

She slid her eyes away and said nothing.

"Get on the train," he urged. "It's our only chance."

Tom walked east through town. He wanted to make sure McCrae hadn't awakened and followed them. He felt relatively certain that the captain, if he came, would come alone; soliciting help from Sherry or a military detail would take too much time and draw too much attention.

Tom walked three blocks, his heels coming down softly on the boardwalk, and turned around. He'd walked a block back toward the station house when a horse that hadn't been there before appeared out of the darkness, tethered to a hitchrack on the opposite side of the street. A warning hammered at the base of his skull, as he slipped his .45 from its holster and started toward the horse. Approaching the animal, Tom saw the sweat glistening on its rump and neck, heard the hoarse wheezing. It had obviously been ridden hard without stopping. Two more steps, and Tom recognized the mount as Anniston McCrae's.

He'd come within a few yards of the horse when he heard a rifle crack. The sound had come from nearby and sent the horse, tired as it was, sunfishing at the hitchrack.

Tom felt a blow to his back so unforgiving it twisted him in a complete circle and sent him sprawling. He knew immediately he'd been shot. He reached for his gun but his right hand wouldn't cooperate. It felt heavy and numb, as though it had been asleep for hours.

He heard a laugh—the cold, unmistakable laugh of Anniston McCrae.

Tom was facing across the street, and he saw the laughing man approach him now from the shadows of an alley. He was carrying a rifle, leveled at Tom. Pale wisps of smoke curled from its barrel. "Well, what a surprise to find my striker in town during the wee hours," McCrae said, with only half-suppressed jubilance. "Did I sign a leave for you?"

"You backshooter!" Tom rasped.

"Don't worry, I'm going to finish you from the front." The barrel of McCrae's rifle went up momentarily as he jacked a shell in the chamber, the spent one falling with a metallic jingle to the street. Then the gun came down again, the octagonal bore widening as it leveled at Tom's eyes.

"It doesn't matter what you do to me," Tom grunted through gritted teeth, "but let Glynette go."

McCrae sighed regretfully. "I'm afraid that won't be possible . . . but look on the bright side. You'll soon be together."

A form moved in the shadows behind Anniston. "Drop the gun, Captain."

Anniston flinched but kept his gun pointed at Tom. He laughed. "Frank, what are you doing here?"

"I was coming to your quarters to stop you, Anniston." Sherry stepped from the shadows, so Anniston could see the gun pointed at him. "I saw the corporal and your wife sneak out of the house. I waited until you followed them."

"I guess you wanted to see me finish off this worthless yellowleg, eh, Captain? The one who broke your nose?"

"No, Anniston. I came to stop my friend from committing murder."

Anniston glared at Sherry from the corner of his eye. "Unless you aim to shoot me, Frank, you'd best get out of here. I'm killing this vermin, then I'm hunting down his concubine and doing the same to her."

Anniston returned his gaze to Tom and slowly squeezed the trigger. "Lights out, Corporal."

A gun barked.

Tom closed his eyes. With the shot, he jerked reflexively, then lay still. He didn't feel the bullet. He half-wondered if he was dead—if it had happened so fast that he was already in the place lone soldiers and aimless drifters went when they died.

He opened his eyes. It hadn't been McCrae's gun that had fired. McCrae still stood over him, but his shoulders were slouched. He dropped his gun, took two clumsy steps forward, and sank to his knees. He tried to say something, but all that passed over his lips was air. Then he pitched forward on his chest, gave a jerk and a sigh, and lay still.

Tom lifted his eyes and saw Captain Sherry, his .45 extended, smoke curling from its barrel. "Glynette," he whispered and closed his eyes.

Epilogue

In mid-October, on a day cool and fresh with the smell of dried leaves and brittle grass, Glynette and Tom rode side by side toward the Antelope Mountains. Glynette had let the breeze lift the hat from her head, and it hung down her back, bouncing on its horsehair cord. Her raven hair blew behind her as she rode the white-footed black mare Orsen Demmer had left for her in Harding, along with Tom's new line-back dun. The two of them rode stirrup to stirrup.

Tom's chin was level, and a tranquil, self-satisfied expression pulled at the corners of his keen eyes. The sun gilded the undulating prairie west of Harding, and redwinged blackbirds wheeled in enormous, web-like flocks from the trees lining the ravines. They'd be heading south soon, leaving the seeds and freeze-dried bugs to winter birds, the nuthatch and the chickadee. Snow had already fallen high in the mountains. Soon it would work its way down to the foothills and the prairie.

"I can't imagine living anywhere else," Glynette said, when they'd pulled up on a ravine lip and gazed over the golds and reds of the foliage tracing the creek below. A golden eagle lifted from a wind-twisted ponderosa pine, heaving its enormous wings toward the opposite ridge, cloaked now in purple afternoon shadow. "It's even more beautiful than I remembered."

"You don't think you'll get homesick for the city?" Tom asked her.

"This is my home now. This big sky and all this land." She smiled at him. "You."

"I hope you still see it that way two months from now," Tom said with a chuckle. "When we're buried in snow."

"I can't think of anything nicer than a long winter under the quilts with you."

Tom grinned. "I don't think I'd mind that myself, Mrs. Flint."

They rode in silence, feeling the bond between themselves and the land deepening. When they reached a shelf above the valley cut through by Elk Creek, they stopped. It was their first view of the creek that cut through their ranch. "When we're both gone—in about sixty years, I mean—" Glynette said, "I want us to be buried together beside Elk Creek."

"We'll have to tell the kids."

"All eleven of them."

Tom lifted a brow.

She shrugged. "We'll need a lot of ranchhands."

Tom laughed and closed his eyes in a moment of thankfulness. He could hardly believe he was here in Montana again, and with Glynette by his side. If Captain Sherry had not shown up when he did, he and Glynette would both be dead. Captain Sherry! What an unlikely hero, but the world was full of mysteries, and for Tom and Glynette, it was enough to know that somehow the drunken Frank Sherry had found the grace and strength to go after Anniston and stop him.

So much had changed since that fateful night. It all seemed like a miracle. Most amazing of all was that

Glynette had insisted, in defiance of all decorum, that they marry in time to return to the ranch before winter. She said she would die if she had to wait until spring, and he had believed her.

They reached the ridge overlooking the Orsen Demmer ranch and reined up. There it was—the low-slung cabin, log barn, and horse corrals sprawling through the hollow. Shadows pooled as the sun burnished the grass and scraggly trees with its copper, late-afternoon glow. Tom spurred his horse down the ridge, following the trail that meandered around boulders and juniper bushes. Glynette followed close behind. When they neared the house, a collie leaped from the porch and took up a vigil of barking.

"Dan!" Tom shouted. "What are you doin' here?" Tom reined up at the hitchrack before the cabin, dismounted, and stooped to rough up his old friend. The door to the cabin opened, and out strode Orsen Demmer, a corncob pipe dangling from his mouth.

"Well, I'll be . . . danged," he said, "if it ain't the two newlyweds."

"How you doin', Dem?" Tom hailed.

"Still kicking, Tom," Dem said, offering a hand to Glynette. "Mrs. Flint—don't that have a nice ring to it?—you look prettier than ever. Marriage to the big galoot must be suitin' you just fine."

"It's wonderful to see you again, Dem," Glynette said, nimbly dismounting her horse. Dem engulfed her in a bear hug that squeezed the air from her lungs. Glynette gave him a heartfelt kiss on his whiskered cheek in return. She couldn't believe it was real, that she was here on the ranch again . . . to stay.

"I'm glad you brought Dan out to see us," Tom said, scratching the collie's ears. The dog grinned happily.

"Well, to tell the truth of it, Dan was hoping he could

stay here with you. The boys said he's been kinda lonesome since you left."

"Is that so?" Tom regarded the dog skeptically, trying to conceal his pleasure. He turned to Glynette. "Do you mind?"

"Do I have a choice?" She bent down to greet Dan. He planted a paw on each of her shoulders and slathered her face with his tongue.

"Dan, you fool," Tom said, pulling the dog away from her.

"He sure knows how to make his case." Glynette stood and scrubbed her face dry on Tom's sleeve.

Clapping a hand on Tom's shoulder, Dem gestured toward the pastures before them. "Well, at long last, this place is your problem now. And not a minute too soon. My old bones can't take another winter here. Tomorrow I'm gettin' my tired old"—he glanced at Glynette—"backside . . . on the way to Californy."

"Winter's never bothered you," Tom said. "Why are you in such a hurry?"

"Believe me, I know when three's a crowd!" Dem removed his pipe and winked.

"It's gettin' kind of late in the year to be traveling," Glynette said gently. "Why don't you stay this winter with us? You can keep us company."

Old Dem drew several puffs of his pipe and said musingly, "I appreciate your hospitality, Mrs. Flint. I'll gladly stay as long as the weather holds. I reckon I'll know when it's time to go."

Tom smiled at the man and squeezed his shoulder. "In spite of all your grousing about the winters, Dem, you belong here. And, more important, we need you here."

The old man blinked his eyes but said nothing.

They grilled steaks on his outside fireplace and sat on the porch, bundled up in buffalo robes, watching the stars

Glynette's Corporal

flicker to life in the flawless autumn sky. They moved inside to eat supper and plan the future by the fire until well after dark. Then Dem grabbed a war bag from his room and stepped off the porch into the darkness, bidding them good night.

"Where you goin'?" Tom asked him. He and Glynette were on the porch again, attracted by the starlight flickering above the southern, tree-studded ridge.

"I fixed me a place in the old bunkhouse. Like I said, I know when three's a crowd." He chuckled and disappeared.

When Dem had gone into the bunkhouse and shut the door behind him, the newlyweds sat on the porch swing in silence. Dan lay at their feet. The only sound was the distant yammering of coyotes and the horses snuffling and stomping in the barn. This was what they had each dreamed of, first privately, then in tandem—building a life together on this ranch.

The realization surrounded them like the cool night air. Tonight would begin their new life. They would run this ranch, raise children, and watch the rhythm of the days and seasons unfold together. Neither could quite fathom that their lives had changed so much in a few short summer months, that they had been swept away by something out of their control.

Tom turned to Glynette. "I think he's got a point."

"What?"

"Three would most definitely be a crowd tonight."

"What are you saying?" she whispered huskily.

"I think you know."

She turned her sensuous smile to him. "Aha . . ." She curled around and leaned into his lap. Wrapping her arms around his neck, she burrowed against him, her thick hair covering his chest. "Seein' how I'm always gettin' you shot, Mr. Flint," she intoned, imitating Tom's accent, "I reckon you figure I owe you a sportin' good time."

"Well, a guy takes a couple of bullets for a gal, he figures he deserves some kinda reward."

"I'd be happy to spend the rest of my life rewarding you." She looked into his eyes, her expression suddenly serious. "Oh, Tom, I'm so sorry—"

He put his fingers over her lips and imitated her cultured East Coast accent. "Don't insult me by apologizing."

She pulled his finger away. "Then how about if I just show you how sorry I am?"

She pressed her lips to his, pouring the passion from every nerve in her body and all the love that had been building inside her for a lifetime into the kiss. His mouth opened against hers in concentrated desire, as though nothing existed outside the kiss. She felt his body respond to every nuance of her movement, and when she finally pulled away, her eyes were smoky with desire.

Tom stood, lifting her in his arms. As they crossed the threshold, and he kicked the door closed behind them, she threw back her head and gave a soft laugh, utterly delighted with the world.

J.R. Clarke Public Library
102 East Spring Street
Covington, Ohio 45318